NAILS
AND EYES

KAORI FUJINO, a lifelong resident of Kyoto, is best known for fiction that reimagines tropes from horror, science fiction, Hollywood thrillers, urban legends and fairy tales. She holds an MA in aesthetics and art theory from Doshisha University. In 2013, Fujino was awarded the Akutagawa Prize, Japan's most prominent literary prize, for *Nails and Eyes*. In the fall of 2017, she was in residence at the University of Iowa's prestigious International Writing Program. Her stories have appeared in English translation in *Granta*, *Monkey* and the *US-Japan Women's Journal*.

KENDALL HEITZMAN is an associate professor of Japanese literature and culture at the University of Iowa. He has translated stories and essays by Nori Nakagami, Tomoka Shibasaki, and Yusho Takiguchi. He is the author of *Enduring Postwar: Yasuoka Shotaro and Literary Memory in Japan* (Vanderbilt University Press, 2019). His translation of "The Little Woods in Fukushima" by Hideo Furukawa appears in *Monkey* magazine, vol. 3 (2022).

KAORI FUJINO

NAILS AND EYES

Translated from the Japanese by

KENDALL HEITZMAN

PUSHKIN PRESS

Pushkin Press
Somerset House, Strand
London WC2R 1LA

First published in the Japanese language as NAILS AND EYES
(爪と目, "Tsume To Me") by SHINCHOSHA
Publishing Co., Ltd. in Tokyo in 2013

First published by Pushkin Press in 2023

Series Editors: David Karashima and Michael Emmerich
Translation Editor: Elmer Luke

Pushkin Press would like to thank the Yanai Initiative for Globalizing
Japanese Humanities at UCLA and Waseda University for its support

3 5 7 9 8 6 4 2

ISBN 13: 978-1-78227-954-9

Designed and typeset by Tetragon, London

Printed and bound by Clays Ltd, Elcograf S.p.A.

www.pushkinpress.com

CONTENTS

NAILS
AND EYES

"I can't marry you." That's what my father told you on the first day of his affair with you. You were so surprised all you could say was, "Oh." My father went on, with what seemed to be genuine regret, that he had a wife and child. "Oh," you replied again. You didn't really care one way or the other. At just that moment, a fleck of mascara had dislodged from your eyelash, slipped into your right eye and got under your contact lens. You squeezed your eyes shut, then opened them wide, then bent forward, blinking repeatedly. But it still stung, so there was nothing to do but remove the contact lens from your eye. You had worn hard lenses since junior high. During the time it took you to hold the lens up to the light, give it a quick lick and get it back into your eye—all with a practised hand—my father kept on talking. "I have a child," he repeated. "She's still a little girl."

"OK, I understand," you said. You said it to let him off the hook, because my father clearly wanted to stop talking about it. But what you really wanted to say was, *It's none of my business whether you have a child or not.*

But a year and a half later, after everything had changed and my father broached the subject of marriage, you warmed to the fact that he had a little girl, because you had kind of started to want one. You were in your mid-twenties at this point, and your friends had started to have babies. But pregnancy seemed like a total burden to you. One of your friends was deemed to be high risk for a miscarriage and spent three months confined to a hospital bed. When you went to visit her, she was lying flat on the bed. She wasn't allowed even to sit up, apparently. You looked down at her face stripped of its make-up, her scraggly eyebrows. Her arm with the IV drip was so puffy it looked like it would burst.

"It's so itchy I can hardly stand it," your friend said, laughing through her ordeal.

You stood there and imagined how you were going to suffer when you got pregnant. You didn't know when your turn would come, but this is the way pregnancy has ravaged women since the dawn of time. And still does. And always will. And unless you made up your mind to refuse all of this, your body would be ravaged, too. But you didn't *actually* think this, of course. It was so plainly obvious that there was really no need for anyone to consciously think it. What you really thought was how uninterested you were in getting pregnant at this point, and how convenient it was that someone else had given birth to the child. Meaning me. I was three years old. Which pleased you, bringing back memories of when you were little and how you had wanted a dog, or a cat, or a bird. Your parents had no interest in animals and held firm, but they weakened when you begged for a hamster. "Hamsters don't make too much noise," your parents had reasoned.

You were small at the time, but the hamster was smaller. So small it was hard for you to believe a pet could be that small. You would pinch its twitchy hind feet together, and lift them up to see if those little pink pads really did belong to a living creature and the whole thing wasn't just some mechanical wind-up toy. The hamster died after four months. You had never cleaned its cage. Your parents offered to buy you a new hamster.

"Naw, that's all right," you said.

"Really?"

"Really."

One of your parents, you can't remember which, placed a hand on your head and said that you should just let them know if you change your mind. Lying on your stomach on the floor, you peered into the cage. The hamster wasn't there any more, so the exercise wheel and tunnel and water bottle all belonged to you. When you tired of imagining yourself having shrunk down to hamster size and playing on all the fun things and curling up to sleep in the hamster hideaway, the cage became just a place to stack your notebooks and textbooks. It took a full year for your mother to realize that you hadn't kept the cage out of fondness for the hamster, but simply because no one had bothered to throw it out. After she got rid of it, you were pleased. "Oh, my room is so much bigger now," you said, letting your backpack slide from your shoulders to the floor.

When my father said to you, "She's really a sweet-tempered, quiet girl," your fingertips were tracing the stem of the teacup. It reminded you of the supple curve of the hamster's twiggy legs. "Hina's not fussy—she'll eat anything—and she doesn't have any allergies," my father went on, referring to me, his only child, and in that brief flicker of time, all your memories of the hamster disappeared.

"I sound like a father, I know, but, honestly, she has very good manners for her age. She's just such a good girl. She's a little confused about everything right now, all that's happened. But, you know, give it a little time and..."

My father wanted you to just move in, take it day by day—no need to overthink anything. Of course he was thinking he wanted to marry you somewhere along the line, but for now you could just move in, and then you could decide whether or not it was working out. True, if you waited *too* long to figure it out, he said, that might be a problem, "If you consider how tough it would be for a little girl."

My father was in his late thirties at the time, so there was an age gap between the two of you, but nothing that anyone would gawk at. And he had a good job at a company that was quite well known to people who knew the industry. What he wanted was someone to take care of things at home and to take charge of his little girl. Meaning, if you moved in, you wouldn't need to work.

You were a temp at this point. You didn't love your job, but you didn't hate it, either. The ups and downs of the job weren't big enough to make you love it or hate it. You went to work every day because there had never been an option *not* to go to work, but it wasn't that painful. Or if it was, it was a pain that you just had to get used to, like the one that came from sticking hard contact lenses into your dry eyes every day.

But the moment the actual possibility of not having to work was dangled right in front of you, the thought of going in the next day suddenly seemed like a very dreary prospect. Going to the office had always been a drag, but never to this extent. A tingling started in your legs, and soon your whole body wanted out of this job. The vibe at work had not been good lately, but you weren't one to do anything to make it better. You knew from experience things were only going to get worse. The teacup in your hand was almost empty, but it suddenly felt heavy. When you set it down, it clanged into the saucer.

"How about six months?" you said. "Let's try living together for six months. And then I'll decide."

My father nodded. He was smiling.

And with that, going to work was no longer the slightest burden. No, now you thought it was wonderful. Because work was now in the past. Even the things that technically belonged to the future—giving notice, clocking in until your last day—all of that was in "the past".

What you really looked forward to, more than living with my father, was living with me. You have a younger brother, but when he was a child, so were you. Since you became an adult, you had not had a single child anywhere near your orbit. A few times, my father brought me along to get to know you, and each time I was quiet and well behaved—exactly as my father had promised. I didn't speak unless I was spoken to. I replied to questions in my tiny, clear voice. You gazed at my spindly neck and wrists. You thought of me as something of an animal.

Yes, I am an animal—the same as you.

You thought that raising my father's child would be valuable practice for raising your own child someday. You stopped by your parents' house on your day off to tell your mother what you had decided to do.

"But don't tell Dad anything just yet," you said to her.

"Well, I suppose that's OK, but. . ." There was dread in your mother's response.

"I mean, this might not lead anywhere. If we decide to get married, we can tell him then."

"Yes, but. . ."

Your mother didn't approve, but she knew that you weren't the type of daughter to care what her parents thought about anything. The days when they could say no to you and expect you to cry and scream and then comply had come to an end when you were in junior high. Your mother called your brother, who was going to college in another prefecture.

"Your sister says that we should keep it a secret from your father."

"Aw, just let her do things the way she wants to," he said.

Your mother gave up the fight soon enough. She knew from the start that she wouldn't get anywhere with you.

She was intimidated by her own daughter. But when she heard that my father had asked for your help raising me less than two months after my mother's death, it dawned on her: "You were having an *affair*!"

"If you want to put it that way, yeah. But I didn't plan to steal him away from his wife. We were just dating," you said, laughing with embarrassment.

My mother died in an accident. At least, it was an accident from all appearances. Not even my father knew what really happened. My father's work had posted him in a different city, two hours away by bullet train. Every two weeks he'd return to the apartment where my mother and I had stayed behind. But then he met you in the city where he worked, and in order to spend more time with you, often he did not come home as planned. He would make excuses that seemed plausible enough: *I have to work straight through my days off*, or *I have to go drinking with the guys from the office*, or *I think I'm coming down with something, so I'd better stay here and sleep it off*. You never knew what my mother thought when that happened. My father never said anything to you about it, and it never occurred to you to ask. You were indifferent to whoever my father's wife happened to be. You never dreamed you would come into possession of me, so you were indifferent to his child as well. Sometimes you would forget whether

I was a girl or a boy. None of this is to say that you weren't indifferent to my father too. You showed no interest in learning about his work, or which teams he rooted for, or what movies or music he liked, or what he had been like as a boy. Not that you were against knowing about these things. If my father started talking about something, you would listen, use the appropriate cues to show you were listening and ask the appropriate questions for him to continue his story. But if my father didn't initiate the conversation, you didn't bother to start one.

My father was the same way. The two of you had a lot in common.

You met my father at an eye clinic where you were both patients. You had done damage to your corneas by wearing your contact lenses for too many hours a day. My father didn't have any problems with his vision, but he had a case of allergic conjunctivitis, brought on by hay fever. It was just the two of you in the reception room, but you found yourselves waiting a long time. You were wearing a pair of ridiculously large black-framed glasses that didn't suit your face at all, and you were passing the time flipping through a fashion magazine. My father's eyes were bloodshot, and he was pulling tissue after tissue out of the box on the low-slung table and wiping his nose. You were called into the examination room first. When my father was called in, you were seated in a chair wearing a pair of those clunky optical trial frames they use to determine your prescription. The nurse was in front of you, leaning slightly in and switching lenses in and out of the slots. The trial frames were perfectly round and even less flattering than the glasses you had been wearing earlier. At a moment when the nurse was sliding a different lens into the slot, you looked out of the corner of your eye at my father and flashed a smile, just a slight curl upward at the corners of your mouth. And seeing your smile, my father realized that he had been staring at you with a dumb smile on his own face.

"You can have a seat over there," the nurse said to my father, nodding to the other examination chair. Your face disappeared from view behind the nurse's back. My father sat down, and idly looked straight ahead at the eye chart's rows of diminishing rings with notches randomly cut out of them. Even without the light behind the translucent panel turned on, he was able to identify the direction of the gaps in the rings pretty deep into the chart. I can do that, too, actually. My eyesight is fantastic. It's probably my father's genes. I wouldn't know what my mother's eyesight was like.

My father went back to the eye clinic the following week. It was a suite in a commercial building. You happened to be in the lift when he stepped into it—again wearing those giant black-framed glasses, but with your shoulder-length hair cinched in back and a light pink cardigan draped over your shoulders. You were clutching your wallet and your mobile phone between your hands. You were much shorter than my father initially thought. And yet, the neck that you were showing off was more stocky than slender. My father got off on the eye-clinic floor. You did not. Just before the door closed, you smiled and bowed, slightly, without looking directly at him. Once again my father realized that you were simply responding to him, because he had turned back to smile at you.

You were working for a mail-order company located in the same building. The third time my father visited the clinic, his symptoms had nearly cleared up, and you were no longer wearing your glasses when he stepped into the lift. It was going down, crammed with people. You raised your eyes, coyly, without lifting your head, to look up at my father, when he realized who you were. He also realized, when your eyes met, that he had been staring at your ears, peeking out from your long hair.

You weren't a beauty queen, you were moderately attractive, but you had the kind of allure that men responded to—and you knew you had it. Your sexual antennae were fine-tuned to detect the slightest interest from a man. And from there you never missed your mark. It was as easy as smushing bugs on a potted plant with your fingertips. You weren't the type to feel a burning desire for something you didn't have, and whenever something did land in your clutches, you took what you could get from it and let it go. No need for anything that cramped your style, and no need for anything unreasonably passionate. That was love to you.

During college and the not-quite-two years that you were a full-time company employee, you acquired something of a sordid reputation. At the mail-order company where you were worked as a temp, you once again started tongues wagging. To the other women in the office, it was outrageous—incomprehensible, that both a married man in his mid-thirties and a college part-timer in his early twenties would invent reasons to linger longingly at your desk and try to impress you, of all people. You were a little less obvious than the men, but it was clear to the women that you simply couldn't decide which one to choose. Or rather, which one you should choose first. Based on the blowback you got from that entanglement, you weren't about to let word get out when things started up with my father.

You were breezing your way through life, with no sense of the toll of time. There were always going to be people who loved you and people who hated you, no matter what you did, so why let anything trouble you? You felt that your life would always be this way. Not as one day going by, and then another, but life as an ever-expanding single day. And yet, time did go by. You extended your temp contract. There was a natural disaster that consumed the entire country. You learned about it from a news bulletin on television. Your co-workers were shaken, horrified by the tragedy, and when you were among them, you were shaken and horrified too. But when you were alone, the emotions vanished. You weren't particularly fearful for yourself. You supposed that at some point—maybe not now, but at some point—the same kind of calamity might happen to you. But actually, even that wasn't your own thought. A co-worker had come up with it. You had just agreed with it. "That's right," you said. "So scary," you said. Because you were expected to. Fear rolled right off of you. Fear was like a pet to you: something you picked up to get a better look at, but that you soon tired of.

Life went on. My father suffered another bout of seasonal allergic conjunctivitis, and as before he needed to visit the eye clinic for several weeks running. By chance you ran into a guy you'd known in college, and you spent the night with him twice. Your grandfather died in hospice care. Something close to civil war broke out in a faraway country that you couldn't locate on a map, and in another faraway country, there was a disaster on a scale similar to the one experienced here. A manga that you had read obsessively during junior high finally finished its run. And, somewhere along the line, my mother died.

It was my father who found my mother's body. He had not planned on coming home that weekend because of a project at work. That actually was the truth. You had gone back to your parents' home because a friend from high school was getting married. So when the project keeping my father on the job unexpectedly fell off the schedule, he hopped on the bullet train and headed home, without calling my mother beforehand. His tactic was to return home whenever he had a chance, even for a short amount of time, to keep my mother from getting suspicious. It was a frigid Sunday morning, so cold that even with a coat on, he could feel his muscles constrict. It showed real dedication to the family to make the trip home in weather like this, my father was convinced. He arrived close to noon. All was quiet. The lights in the apartment weren't on, but the heat was turned up high. Standing in the entryway, he could feel warm air flowing out. He removed his gloves and coat.

He found me in the bedroom he shared with my mother, in the middle of their double bed, face down, fast asleep. He brought his head close to listen to my breathing. Then he went into the living room, picked up the remote control for the wall-mounted heating unit, and lowered the temperature a few degrees. My mother was nowhere to be found. The lace curtains over the sliding glass doors to the balcony had been pulled shut, and the heavier drapes over them left partway open, allowing some light into the room. The bottom half of the sliding doors was frosted glass, so one's eyes naturally went to the clear glass on the upper half of the doors. My mother always said she loved the wonderful view that came with living on a high floor of the building, but from where my father was looking, near the dining table, he couldn't see anything like a "wonderful view". The sky was simply a hazy glow, like a sheet of patternless wallpaper.

When my father tried my mother's mobile phone, wondering where she was, he was jolted by the jangle of a ringtone right next to him. The phone was lying on the chair at the dining table where she always sat. My father was perplexed. He turned on the lights, opened the fridge and grabbed a bottle of mineral water. There were dishes in the sink: a glass with traces of milk and a plate with a scattering of breadcrumbs. He went to the

demonstrated by turning the crescent-shaped lever. My cheeks were flushed; I was agitated by the fact that something very unusual was happening. My mother's death was ruled an accident. No one ever told me exactly how my mother died.

I don't remember what her voice sounded like. What I remember is her smile. Mama laughed, and I laughed with her. With our mouths close to the glass of the door that separated us, it soon clouded up. We thought that was so funny, but as we kept laughing, our breath clouded up the glass even more and made it difficult for us to see each other, so we needed to do everything we could to stop laughing. I stood up on my tiptoes and tilted my head back as far as it would go and looked up at Mama. With sunlight spreading through the clouded glass, Mama looked like a jumble of spare parts. The white collar of her blouse, the thin grey cardigan wrapped around her shoulders, the fingers that poked out of the sleeves like timid little animals. Those fingers were making a curving motion over and over again, and pointing at something just below them, while at the same time her mouth, never losing that kind smile, formed shapes slowly and painstakingly. So many shapes.

Your own mother's various theories all pointed to it being a suicide due to my father's infidelity. The more she thought about it, the more she convinced herself. She felt she had to say something to you, but it was too difficult to broach. When she finally did, her voice was shaking and tears were falling.

You responded with a sardonic smile. "Oh, please, his wife didn't know a thing about us," you said bluntly. "Nobody knew about us. And marriage was the last thing on my mind."

How could you be so sure that she didn't know, your mother wondered. Yet there was no evidence that my mother knew anything. She had never said a word to anyone, never voiced any suspicion. Her parents were dead. She had an older brother who lived far away with a family of his own, but it had been at least five years since they had talked on the phone or exchanged emails. She didn't leave behind a diary or any letters. So if it was suicide, perhaps she felt that raising a child practically on her own was suffocating her, or maybe she was gripped by depression, or maybe she suddenly had a death wish, the way some people fall in love at first sight.

Your mother also worried about the child my mother left behind. Whatever had really happened, surely I was no longer normal. I was a child who had suffered a grievous trauma, and if someone didn't help me, I would soon be a child dragged under. Your mother couldn't imagine that she herself would be able to shoulder the burden of such a child. But hers weren't the shoulders in question. It was yours that the burden would fall on.

"Please get the girl into counselling. And please, whenever you go out on the balcony, make absolutely sure you have your mobile phone on you. If that woman had just had her mobile phone on her, maybe. . . right?" You replied, "OK, yeah."

After a moment, your mother tried again, this time attempting to give the situation a sunnier view. "I'm sure everything will be fine. You're giving it a six-month trial period, and if it doesn't work out. . ."

"Exactly. It's not like we're getting married right away or anything," you said ever-so-casually. "What's really great about the girl is that even though she's only three, right after dinner she goes and brushes her teeth without needing to be told. That's good training. Don't you think? She had a good mother."

In that moment, your mother despised you. She recalled all the times she had felt a violent hatred of you. You held out a box of tissues, and your mother took one and blew her nose. If nothing was getting through to you, she could at least kick you in the shins: "It's always somebody else's problem, isn't it? Everyone else gets hurt, but nothing bad ever happens to you." She somehow managed to make it sound encouraging and threatening all at the same time, halfway between *So I'm sure everything will be fine* and *But it won't always be that way.*

Your mother saw the benefits of both scenarios. She hoped you would have a quiet, happy life, and at the same time, she hoped you would suffer setbacks, exhaustion and failure. You put the box of tissues down and extended a wastebasket.

From all appearances, my mother's death damaged me. At first, my father tried to hire a babysitter, but he quickly realized the limitations of that.

After the police investigation, I wouldn't go anywhere near the balcony. I refused even to look at it, meaning I could no longer go into the living room or into my own room, which I could only get to by going through the living room. If anyone tried to get me to go there, I would scream and cry. It was a strange sort of crying. I didn't bawl. I simply stood with my mouth wide open as tears poured down my face. I made a sound somewhere between an *ahh* and an *ohh*, and didn't stop until I was out of breath. My cry maintained a steady pitch that sounded less human than like a pipe with a broken seal spewing air. And so my father kept the door to the living room closed and limited my life to the portion of the apartment closest to the entryway: the main bedroom, the toilet and the bath. My father and the babysitter had to bring me meals in the bedroom.

I bit my nails. My father noticed it on his own—he didn't need the babysitter to alert him to it. Whenever he and I were alone, the constant *chk-chk* of me chewing on my nails broke the silence of the house. I was always slobbering on them, my fingertips perpetually ice cold.

"Stop that, please," he would say, and I would pull my fingers out of my mouth, but it was never long before the *chk-chk* of my teeth gnashing at my nails would start up again. Sometimes I would nibble too far down and draw blood. When I bled, my fingers would get even colder. Until my father grabbed my hands and yanked them out of my mouth, I would suck on the blood, not showing any sign of pain, and continue to raze my way across the nails. As my father watched me, it dawned on him that I had to be swallowing fragments of my fingernails. My father had never bitten his nails, and he now worried that his daughter's stomach would be damaged by the shards of fingernails piling up in there. A doctor reassured him that there was no cause for concern about that. Granted, she should stop because it was unhygienic, the doctor explained, but shouting at her or slapping her hands would only be counterproductive.

"The first thing to do is to remove whatever is making her feel unsettled," the doctor pronounced.

After you agreed to try living with us, my father asked for permanent reassignment to the city where he had met you on his temporary posting. The company took what had happened into account and swiftly approved his request. My father put our apartment up for sale. His plan was to use the proceeds from the sale to purchase a single-family home. A house would be better than an apartment if I was going to forget my birth mother. But he couldn't find a buyer for our apartment.

"Right now, I don't see how we can buy a house," he said to you, talking so fast that it sounded like he was making excuses.

"Well, so much for that," you said.

My father signed a lease for an apartment with a reasonable rent. "Once the old place sells, we can go house-hunting," he said. He was trying to cushion your disappointment, put a positive spin on things. But you weren't disappointed in the least.

"And anyway, we're not getting married right away. I want you to really think things through over the next six months. So when you think about it that way, maybe not buying a house right away is actually the right move."

"Sure," you said, a response open to interpretation. You

were thinking about a wedding. You hadn't talked about anything wedding-related with my father, but you had the feeling that he didn't particularly want one. Considering that my father already had a child, your parents probably weren't so eager for a wedding, either. But, you thought, how sad not to have a wedding. Then you realized that you didn't have any friends you wanted to show off to in a wedding dress. You didn't even know if you could call your friends from college or from work your friends any more. Every once in a while you would have email exchanges, and on really rare occasions you would meet up. If you were invited to their weddings, you dutifully went to them. You imagined how you might be sad if you were to lose all of those people from your life. But sadness, like fear, rolled right off of you; it wasn't anything that would seep into your core. You had a moment of self-awareness—possibly the first time *that* had happened in your life—which made you smile: it was kind of fun to imagine things that you wouldn't consider any great loss being dramatically taken from you.

You didn't give your co-workers at the mail-order company any reason for your departure. A few people tried to ferret it out of you, but you learned that when you said that "things will be very different at home now" and looked down, it effectively ended the conversation. Any further questioning would appear inappropriate. You left a giant tin of cookies in the office kitchenette as a goodbye token and moved into the three-bedroom apartment my father had found. Of all the friends whose contact information was saved in your mobile phone, you didn't text a single one to say that you had moved.

This time around, it was decided that my bedroom would be next to the entryway. My father and I moved in two days ahead of you, but here again, I didn't show any inclination to set foot into the combined dining-and-living area, given that the living room opened to the balcony. The furniture and appliances had been shipped from the previous apartment, right down to the living-room curtains, which survived the relocation on the dubious merit of just happening to be exactly the right size. The only thing missing was a bed for the adults.

"I've been sleeping on the sofa for the last two nights," my father said, rather proud of himself.

"Why would you do that?" you replied. He seemed a little caught off guard.

He told you to buy whatever you wanted for the place and handed you his credit card, and you bought a bed that caught your eye at a home-furnishings store in the neighbourhood. You bought sheets, a duvet, and a cover for the duvet. You had brought me along with you. I was quiet and submissive. My mother had trained me well, after all. There was a full selection of duvet covers in their plastic cases before us. "Which colour should we get?" you asked, but I didn't reply. It didn't appear to register with you that I hadn't said a word. "Mmm hmm," you said, and went with the beige one.

After that, we happened to go by the curtains. You ambled down the aisle running your fingers across the models on display, but something stopped me in my tracks. You were near the end of the aisle by the time you turned around and sauntered back to me. "What did you find?" you asked me. Pointing to the curtain in front of me, I said, "Pink." Giving the curtain a tug, you said, "Yep, that's pink."

Despite how cheap the hot pink curtains looked once they were hanging in our living room, they were actually high-quality ones designed to block out the light. When they were completely closed, my father felt the room became so oppressive that it was hard to breathe. But when he came home and saw me sitting at the dining table quietly biting my nails and staring at the curtains in the living room, and you sitting across from me flipping through a magazine, he made the tactical decision not to say anything.

When the sliding glass doors were closed and the pink curtains were drawn, I was calm as could be. It was clear that I wanted nothing to do with the living room, but I had no qualms about wandering in and out of the dining area, and so a lot of the logistical concerns for daily living were eased.

You also bought a collapsible laundry-drying rack for use indoors, together with a dehumidifier. When you told your mother about this over the phone, she had her reservations. "Is that... well, that's good, these are... particular circumstances," your mother started. She wanted her daughter to know about the sterilizing powers of direct sunlight and natural breezes. But her daughter, always a step ahead of her and with zero interest in hearing what was sure to be a lecture on traditional laundry techniques, pre-empted any such discussion. "It doesn't matter where you hang things; drying is drying," you said, wrapping the call up.

When you used the collapsible drying rack, it had to be placed diagonally across the living room in order to fit. That made the room look cluttered, but you weren't in the least concerned about that. I stared with fascination at the rack, this sort of flying contraption that had spread its wings to fill the living room. Whenever it was opened there, it seemed to claim control over the space and to force us into the dining area. Here, where the outside world didn't exist for us, we shared the space silently, completely naturally, without any concern for each other, without tension. It was as though we had lived together as a family our entire lives... or as though we were total strangers who happened to sit down near each other in a public place.

You made enquiries at the nearest preschool, hurriedly filled out the paperwork and managed to get me admitted before the annual entrance ceremony. Every day you took me to school and picked me up, made sure I changed clothes and ate, put me in the bath and tucked me in for the night. But, really, as my father said, I had been brought up to take care of myself as much as possible, so all you needed to do was prompt me to do these things. I had less and less to say, but I obeyed, silently. You tried to win me over with junk food. My mother had allowed me almost nothing processed or unhealthy, so I was immediately on board. You doled out salty snacks. You kept the juice and chocolate coming. As long as I was shoving things into my mouth, there was no need for you to speak with me. Plus, the more I ate, the less I chewed on my nails—not because it was helping me address the underlying causes of the habit, but simply because I couldn't gnaw on snacks and my nails at the same time. As far as my father was concerned, this was good enough. Because I had stopped my crying jags too, he felt that he had made the right decision having you move in.

But that's not to say that my father felt that you were good at housekeeping. His dead wife had had a passion for order and cleanliness; she was the ideal homemaker. You, on the other hand, were not. When my father came home from work, the laundry would be strewn like wreckage across the sofa and on the rug in front of it. There was no recognizable pattern you followed in folding underwear or socks. My father's dead wife had always prepared the time-honoured well-rounded meal—three dishes of varying sizes, soup and rice—whereas you made one dish, heaped on a large plate to share, and a small basic salad. And often you would buy a ready-made dish at the supermarket and simply slide it onto a plate. After dinner was done, you offered me more cheap sweets as dessert, right in front of my father. *I'm not going to worry about that*, my father decided. Somehow, with the way that I innocently craved sweets, I had started to seem like a child again. Once the marriage was signed and sealed, he would point things out and push for a few improvements. My father couldn't bear to lose you. He was afraid of how young you were. He knew that you could be impulsive. His plan was to get you pregnant as soon as possible.

Things didn't go according to plan.

* * *

After my mother died, my father had trouble performing in bed with you. "It's because of what happened. That's how deeply it hit me," my father said.

"I'm sure," you replied. My father was relieved that you weren't going to hold this against him. He was even optimistic, believing the move to a new apartment and the start of a new living situation would help things down there spring back to life. But that was too much to expect. Even when he pulled you close in the bed that you had picked out, his hand sliding across your stomach and around to your hip, nothing.

My father was thinking about his wife's eyelids when he found her on the balcony. They had been almost entirely closed. There may have been a sliver of the whites of her eyes visible in the gap between her lids and her lower eyelashes, but he was no longer sure. What stayed with him was how paper-thin the flesh of her eyelids appeared in death. He realized that what he had always thought of as a simple layer of skin covering the eyes actually contained fat and muscle like anywhere else on the body. But her eyelids had gone slack over the eyeballs beneath, revealing every grisly contour. Where the eyes should have bulged in the centre, they were caving in. That was what he remembered about finding my dead mother.

Your eyelids, as he looked at them now from close range, were full and vital. As you blinked, your moist eyes appeared and disappeared. When you used to meet up at a hotel, there had been hard contact lenses in those eyes. Around your brown irises, a faint shimmering halo. Here at home in your own bed, there was none of that. You were just going to sleep after this, so your contacts were already out.

"Can you see it?" my father asked, pulling back from you a bit.

"See what?" You peered at my father, hovering over you.

"My face."

"Your face?"

"Yes, my face."

You weren't easily flustered in conversations. Your response was like silk.

"I can see you have a face."

"What is that supposed to mean?"

"I can't make out every detail. I can see you have eyes and a nose and a mouth, but I can't tell exactly what they look like. It's all super fuzzy."

You talked as though it was no big deal, but my father was baffled by this. To you, wasn't he just like one of those creepy spirits that seem human but really have no facial features?

My father hadn't realized until you came to live with us that your vision without contact lenses was barely 20/200. He couldn't grasp what that meant. But I can. Because my vision is incredibly good. So good that I can even fully imagine what it must be like to be extremely nearsighted like you. It was beyond my father's comprehension how those eyes of yours, which couldn't see anything clearly, were able to lock in on his at all. My father didn't put too much stock into the notion that eyes were the window to a person's soul, but even he felt that the eyes, compared to other organs, had something more going for them. And yet, the longer he looked into your eyes, glazed with a thin veneer of tears, restlessly whirring into motion, the more he wondered if there was nothing more to eyes than their function. Whether they were moist, however they moved, none of it had to do with emotions or sensuality. Eyes were moist because to function as sensory organs they needed moisture, and they moved because as sensory organs they needed to move to do their job. What my father was gazing down into were two small organs fed by a network of blood vessels.

When my father eventually apologized for his latest failed attempt and climbed off of you, you were somehow deflated, but you didn't betray any sadness or disappointment. My father thought about the first time he encountered you at the eye clinic. How you had looked at him out of the corner of your eye while you were being fitted with lenses. But if you glanced over at my father without any corrective lenses, as had to have been the case, that meant you smiled at him without being able to see a single feature of his face. My father wasn't sure how he should feel about this. There were times when he thought that your smiling blindly at him that day was charming, and there were times when he thought it was somewhat disturbing.

In order to test his machinery, my father took up with other women. He was greatly relieved to find that his parts were still in working order. When he looked at the closed eyes of these other women, he still thought of his dead wife's shrivelled eyelids, and when he looked into the open eyes of these other women, as with yours, all he could see were a pair of optical organs. And yet, it seemed that only with you was he having this kind of trouble.

You sensed right away that my father was sleeping with other women. You didn't have concrete evidence, but your suspicions weren't entirely ungrounded. My father still tried to have sex with you, every once in a while, and although nothing had improved, the anxiety that he had shown earlier was no longer there. Now, it seemed that the tables were turned—each time my father waited for you to show sympathy, to console him. You did as he wished. My father responded with a little sheepishness but at the same time a strange satisfaction as he acted sympathetic to you. His attitude seemed to imply that the problem lay with you and not with him. You realized there was only one way he could have confirmed this.

Despite that, you didn't see the need to dig through his belongings or confront him. You had imagined that infidelity was a part of the bargain, so it was hard to be too broken-hearted about it. On the contrary, you could identify with him. When cheating men see an opportunity, they take it. You had done the same, on any number of occasions. So actually, for the first time, you felt unadulterated affection for my father. It was very similar to the quiet affection that you had for yourself.

Things were a lot easier this way. If my father wasn't going to change the way he had lived to this point, then there was no need for you to change the way you had lived to this point, either.

You grew tired of me. I maintained the silence that my mother had taught me was proper in the presence of guests. I was unnervingly good at this. I did nothing that would require you to provide me instruction. Which was good, because you didn't have anything to teach me.

Was this child always going to be as good as this? you wondered. This led you to think about your future. You were still young. You could, if you wanted, just walk straight out of this apartment and move back in with your parents. You could register with a temp agency or start interviewing at companies to become a salaried employee. There was surely a job for you somewhere. You could meet a new man—or maybe an old flame—fall in love and get married. You had possibilities. I had possibilities, too, and they vastly outnumbered yours. But when I sat there devouring snacks, it was like I was chomping through all of my potential futures before they had a chance to play out.

You found yourself a lover. You didn't go looking for one; he appeared out of the ether.

It all started with the books. At dinner one night, my father suddenly said, "Let's get rid of the books." He was looking into the tatami room. The sliding door was half-open, and a cardboard box was sitting on the threshold, a corner of it poking into the living room. The tatami room had become the de facto storage room; all of the things my father had shipped from the old apartment were crammed in there, together with all of your things.

"If we get rid of the books, it will open up closet space where we can store some of the other things, and then we can start drying clothes there instead of in the living room."

"Books?" you said. There was a bookshelf in the living room. When you arrived it was mostly empty, except for some CDs, DVDs and a few instruction manuals for appliances. You had added some cookbooks and magazines, which had trouble staying up and were usually flopping over. You of course knew it was a bookshelf, but it hadn't occurred to you that such an object had at one time been filled with actual books.

The following day, after my father headed off to work and after you deposited me at preschool, you opened the door to the closet in the tatami room. There were stacks of cardboard boxes filled with my dead mother's books. Novels, foreign picture books for children, cookbooks.

You picked up a hardcover novel. You didn't know or care about the contents, but you liked the feel of it in your hands. You don't read novels. You couldn't remember when you last held a hardcover book in your hands. It was lighter than you would have guessed from looking at it. You tossed the book in your hands a couple of times, riffled through the pages. There was a sewn-in lavender ribbon bookmark, longer than the length of the book itself and folded so as to fit into the book. The bookmark had never been touched; it was still in its original groove, pressed into the pages when the book was made. You delicately lifted it up and pulled it out to its full length, ran your fingertip along the furrow where it had been, tucked it into another page at random and closed the book.

You emptied the entire contents of the boxes onto the living-room floor. The paperbacks were all slightly worn, with discoloured pages, while the hardcovers looked brand-new. On closer inspection, the bookmarks embedded in most of these hardcovers had not been touched. Clearly, these books had never been read. One by one, you opened them, lifting and unfolding the bookmarks, running your fingers over the indentations left on the page. This for some reason led you to brush your fingers over the page numbers and down the lines of text, as though the numbers and words were bits of debris or dead bugs. The paper, never before touched, was soft and quick to absorb the moisture from your fingertips. But as the skin dried out, the grooves in your fingerprints and the fibre of the paper rasped up against each other, leaving both a little worse for the wear.

After you had uprooted all of the bookmarks—a lot of white ones and red ones, but also olive, yellow, blue, pink and lavender ones—you put the books back in the boxes. You didn't need any more cookbooks, and the novels that you'd run your fingers through were of no use to you. You set aside four foreign picture books because you liked their covers. Everything else was stuffed back into the boxes, which you left on the living room floor.

You brought out your laptop and searched online for used bookstores in the area. Right away you found a small shop with a cafe that specialized in art books but handled a few other subjects as well. It appeared to be a fairly well-known place; it got the occasional write-up in lifestyle magazines.

The guy who came to take a look at the books seemed to be roughly your age. His hair was ridiculously long in front, and he dressed like a college student. His once-white canvas trainers were a dull grey. Despite all appearances, he was the owner of the bookstore. You let him into the apartment, but instead of sitting at the table or on the sofa, he sat down cross-legged on the floor and proceeded to go through the boxes right there. You had thought he was just going to take them and be gone; you rushed to make some instant coffee, but then he didn't want any. You sat at the dining table drinking coffee by yourself, sizing up this bookstore man sitting down on the floor with his back to you. He had broader shoulders than my father. The room felt smaller than it usually did. His estimate took a full hour to complete.

"This is a pretty stylish pad," he said when he was done and preparing to cart off the boxes. It was a good thing you had shoved the laundry rack into the tatami room, you thought. Because it was getting close to the time to pick me up from preschool, you left the apartment with him.

The preschool was about twenty minutes away by foot. Most of the mothers would ride a bicycle to and from school, but you and I always walked. When we walked, we acted as though the other one wasn't there. Sometimes you walked ahead of me, sometimes I walked ahead of you. At times, we would happen to walk side by side. The reason we didn't go by bicycle is that you didn't feel confident riding one. When you were young and got on a bicycle with a classmate, you were never the one to pedal. And once, when four of you were riding recklessly on a single bicycle, you'd got into an accident. The bookseller gave you a lift to the preschool in his delivery van.

On days when he didn't have any books to pick up, the bookseller's work generally didn't start until late afternoon. The two of you started meeting while I was at preschool, two or three times a week, always at his apartment. It was a studio apartment, primarily for singles and students. He would answer the door with a bad case of bed-head, wearing a pilly T-shirt and cotton trousers that had seen better days. It never appeared that he had done anything to clean up the place before you arrived.

"Sorry it isn't the kind of fancy apartment you're accustomed to," he said with a laugh. Even his laugh seemed unkempt.

The floor was covered with towering piles of books, with only a single path across it to the bed against the back wall. Some piles were so tall they seemed to quiver as you gingerly made your way past them. "Don't worry, don't worry," the bookseller said, completely unconcerned. "Don't worry" didn't mean "Don't worry, they're not going to fall over." They did, like dominoes. Ever nonchalant, he would reach out with his broad hands to restack them.

"Are you selling these, or are they your own?" you asked him.

"I'm selling them," he said. "But if you see anything you like, feel free to take a couple home with you."

"Um, thanks, but I think I'm good."

"I'm serious. It's really fine."

"I mean, I don't really read books."

"You're kidding."

You and the bookseller looked at each other, smiling. A tremor seemed to ripple across his face—did you really say that, or was he missing something?

"Fine, I'll take one," you said reflexively.

You turned around, looking among the piles of books. But your eyes didn't settle on any one in particular. You were just measuring time in your head. In order to create a realistic impression, you paid careful attention to your breathing and where your eyes went. You hadn't told the bookseller that I wasn't your daughter, or that you weren't married to my father, or that my father had a dead wife. You didn't think any of it had any bearing on your budding relationship with him, so explaining all of it was just too much trouble.

You inched your way around, scanning the spines of two or three stacks, lifting up the book on top of one stack to examine the one directly underneath it. Then you reached out to a stack of paperbacks and carefully slipped out the fourth one from the top. The moment you saw the cover you regretted it. It was almost entirely black, and on the lower half a prairie was depicted by lines that looked as though they had been scratched into the surface with a wire. Worse, it was a little beaten up. There was an actual dent in the cover, maybe caused by a fingernail. The black ink had flaked off the side of the image, exposing the white paper beneath. The edges of the pages had roughly the same yellowish tint as your own fingers.

"This one."

You bent it slightly, your thumb flipping through the pages. This caused a book-sized musty breeze to waft up. Even that was enough to dry out the contact lenses in your eyes. You held the book out for the bookseller to see.

"That one?"

"This one."

"That one was yours. It was part of the lot I bought from you at your apartment."

You turned the cover to look at it again. Now that he mentioned it, it did feel like you had seen it before.

"Right," you replied, nodding. "Let me have it back. I was looking for it. I was wondering if I had sold it to you by mistake."

You slowly slid the book into your bag, then took off your cardigan and placed it over the bag. When the bookseller came to you, the stacks of books shuddered but didn't fall over. In all your visits, the books only ever toppled over when you walked by; it never happened when he moved around.

On days when you were with the bookseller, your trysts ran through the lunch hour, although the two of you never ate together. The kitchen in his apartment showed no sign of use. There was a refrigerator, but it wasn't plugged in. You opened it once; it was stuffed with books. The cafe at his bookstore was run by someone else, but he was usually able to get them to prepare an extra staff meal for him, he explained.

"I'm not really picky when it comes to food," he said. "As long as it fills me up, it's all good. The most important thing is volume."

"Does that apply to books, too?" you asked, quite pleased with yourself.

When you were with your bookseller, you never really felt that hungry either, and you always wanted to be with him until the last possible minute before picking me up, so you just skipped lunch. On those days, you would bring me home and join me for snack time. I always ate more than you did. With single-hearted devotion, I tore into my treats, letting them slide down my throat. You lost a little weight, while I got noticeably chubby. My mother had bought me clothes a size or two too large, so that I could grow into them. I had always been a skinny kid, swimming in my clothes, but now my body plumped up little by little to fill them out. Your eyes registered none of it.

You weren't looking at me; you were looking at the room. It took a comment from the bookseller to make you realize that the furnishings my father had shipped from the old apartment hadn't just been acquired at random. All the furniture in the living room had the same colour palette and reflected a unified sense of style. You ended our snack time, washed your hands and fired up your laptop at the dining table. You learned that the grey-tinged wood was walnut, or perhaps a composite that had been coloured to resemble walnut.

You came to look at the furnishings in my room. In the window there were white curtains with pastel-green stripes. The desk, the bed and the chest of drawers were wood painted white. They were sleek and simple, with no decorative elements. They were things that my father's dead wife had picked out—everything in keeping with her particular taste.

You looked at the pink curtains in the living room, and they suddenly seemed out of place. You went into the bedroom you shared with my father and looked at the bed you'd selected. It was cheap and shabby compared to the walnut dresser that stood next to it. You still had my father's credit card. You went online and ordered a walnut double bed. You purchased a new duvet cover and pillowcases made by a popular Scandinavian design house. You had been vaguely aware the brand existed, but you had never had the slightest interest in it. Now that you were seeing their goods everywhere you went online, though, you desperately wanted what they were selling.

As you searched for ways to redecorate the apartment, you discovered an endless trove of blogs about flawlessly kept private dwellings, usually created by women. Their ages varied wildly, from their twenties to their fifties, and so did their profiles: they were single, or married homemakers, or married and working. Some had children, some didn't. They lived in apartments, or condominiums, or newly constructed single-family homes, or renovated older homes, but whatever their situations, their living spaces were surprisingly of a pattern. Almost all of the homeowners treasured the same Scandinavian dishware, the same Scandinavian bedding, the same "Scandinavian style" furniture—arranged just so—and occasionally they'd throw into the mix a piece of old furniture acquired for the prominent stain or visible damage that was the hallmark of a good "antique".

The walnut furnishings that my father's dead wife had selected were of this same aesthetic. You beckoned me over. Gripping my bag of salty snacks, I got down from my chair and plodded over to yours.

"I'm thinking we should change the curtains in the living room, but which of these do you like?"

I looked at the screen on your laptop for a long time, the *crunch crunch* of my chewing not stopping. It was taking me so long to say a word that you stole a quick glance over at me and saw that on my otherwise expressionless face, tears had welled up in my eyes.

"You like the pink ones we have there now?" you asked. I nodded, as the tears trickled down my face. You took another look around the room. "OK," you said. In some ways, the walnut and the pink curtains created their own palette. I licked the crumbs that remained on my fingers, and chewed on the nail of my pinkie.

The new walnut double bed arrived, and you got rid of the still-new bed from the home-furnishings centre. You bought new tableware. The dishes that my father's dead wife had acquired were all white; in the world of home-furnishings blogs this was a sign of impeccable taste, but for you it was somehow lacking. You ordered plates and cups and saucers with a tangled-vine pattern, which was considered an acceptable alternative by the blogosphere. You bought some ceramic decorative dolls and a small pitcher. These you placed as decorations on the bookshelf. For the four foreign picture books that you kept, you bought a wire bookstand where they could be displayed with their covers facing out. You remembered the paperback that had been sitting in your bag this whole time. It wasn't exactly the kind of cover that merited a front-facing presentation, so you slipped it into the bottom of the bookshelf along with the cookbooks and magazines.

When I returned home after school, I stared hard at the picture books on display, my preschooler's shoulder bag still weighing me down. I gnawed on my thumbnail, bit off a sliver of my middle fingernail and said in a small, squelched voice, "My favourite books."

"Really, Hina? I'm glad we found them," you said.

"I looked for them."

"Really? I'm glad we found them," you repeated.

By the time you had been living with us for two months, the mounds of dirty and clean laundry had been greatly reduced. The collapsible laundry-drying rack was now being used exclusively in the tatami room, removing the biggest eyesore. On the blogs that you followed, there were any number of tips posted regarding the art of storage. You wouldn't be rising to my mother's housekeeping standards anytime soon, but you did your research and learned how to clean and clean up. My father thought that things were moving in the right direction. If you supply her with the right environment, a woman will naturally make herself into a wife and mother. It was happening here! He had selected a woman of such normal instincts, and in her prime. My father was pleased with himself. Looking at things as they now stood, he thought he might not need to give you a child of your own. My father offered no complaints about the purchases you made on your own; actually, he told you to go ahead and purchase more things if you'd like. It never occurred to him that you had a lover. And he had definitely never caught on to the fact that before you moved in, you had a fling with a friend from college. Once a woman gets involved with a man everything about her changes, my father actually believed. He was sure there would be red flags: you would put on more make-up, or wear more risqué clothing, or invest in sexier panties. He believed this even though when you were having an affair with *him*, nothing about you changed in the least. Then again, it makes perfect sense that my father would be so clueless—he never knew what you were like before you started sleeping with him.

You put all of the domestic knowledge you were gaining to good use, even for the bookseller's benefit. You sat completely naked on his bed, buttocks on heels, and pulled out a cold, clammy T-shirt that he had taken off and for whatever reason wedged between the bed and the wall. Half of his shirts seemed to have been abandoned there.

"Look at how wrinkled this is."

"It'll straighten out when I wear it again."

"Obviously, what you're supposed to do is fold these and store them on end in a drawer, like files in a filing cabinet."

"Obviously."

You leaned your upper body forward and began to demonstrate how to fold the T-shirt. The bookseller only had eyes for your naked back.

Over the past two months, you had accumulated a number of saved tabs on your internet browser. It was a huge task to keep up with all of the blogs, including scrolling down through all of their previous posts, but you performed it dutifully with me sitting across from you munching on my snacks. And you did it with a liberal use of eye drops. What appeared before your bleary eyes was a carefully curated accumulation of moments in time. One blogger announces her pregnancy, while another has just given birth. Others have sons and daughters entering college, or graduating. Although not at the same frequency at which children get mentioned, there are details of husbands' interests and activities, and numerous reports of the deaths of parents and parents-in-law. The bloggers retire, change jobs, get promotions, are reassigned, take vacations and occasionally move. A number of blogs start up, while a number go silent— sometimes with a message explaining the lack of new posts, other times without a single word of explanation. In these cases, it's possible the blogger has died. At the very least, that was the case with one of your favourites: my mother's blog.

You had no idea what my mother looked like. You didn't know how tall she was, or what her body was like. You guessed that she had to be older than you, but you didn't know by how much. You knew her name—my father had mentioned it. It was Kana. But you didn't know which kanji she used to write it. You knew the kanji for my name, Hina, and you assumed that the *na* in my name would be the same as hers. But that was all you knew.

It didn't really matter, the kanji in her name, what she looked like, how old she was. My mother hadn't wanted people to know any of that. What you found in the blog was the version of my mother that she did want people to know. You had started out from one of the blogs that you visited daily, clicked your way from link to link, and there it was: "Crystal-Clear Days". The blog consisted mainly of photos with text that ran no more than one or two lines per post.

When you first discovered it, your ears were full of the sound of my teeth demolishing a salty snack. Then a glugging sound. You tilted the screen on the laptop down towards you to see what was happening. I was drinking something sugary. The carbonation was strong, but I gulped it down. Normally, if it was water, you would never see me drink like that. You were amazed a child could do that. For someone who had only been swallowing for three years, I had a powerful gullet.

I wiped my mouth with the back of my hand and looked at you. I maintained eye contact as my hand fished another piece out of the snack bag and shoved it into my mouth.

"Do you like those?" you asked. You laughed in a friendly way.

"Yes." I remained expressionless.

"There's more," you said, getting up from the table. You came back with another bag from the snack stock and set it in front of me.

You turned back to your laptop and scrolled down in a frenzy through the blog you had just found. You compared the furnishings on your screen with the furnishings in the apartment. You finally brought yourself to check the name of the blogger, as if you needed any more proof: hina*mama. New posts had stopped appearing the previous autumn. My dead mother had been alive until the previous autumn. The very last post was a photo of purple clouds dotting the sky, looking like little birthmarks. The text read: "I love how the sky looks from my balcony. The only thing missing is an umbellata."

The day that my mother died, her laptop was not to be found in our apartment. She had been using the same computer since before she married my father, and it had stopped working three weeks before she died. My father hadn't known that. He'd only found out from the police, who had questioned other residents of our building and learned about the computer from some of the other mothers there with children my age. The laptop had been disposed of, handed over to one of those roaming trucks that take away old electronics for free. She didn't buy a new one.

There was still a digital camera in the house. It was a compact type; my dead mother had picked it out, and my father bought it. My father didn't know what kind of photos my mother had taken with it, because she never told him and the memory card was missing. My father wasn't much of one to take photos, and you weren't in the habit, either, except for those times when you would take a quick snap of something with your mobile phone instead of writing it down. So the digital camera emptied of its memories had stayed where it was, buried in one of the cardboard boxes in the closet of the tatami room.

"Crystal-Clear Days" had a lifespan of about two years; new posts had been added around four times a month. Here was a photo of the very dining table where your laptop was sitting, where I was even now dropping fragments of my snack from my mouth and fingers, about which she had written, "I finally bought the dining table that I have been wanting to get for so long!" Here was the bookshelf that you had decorated with Scandinavian dishes and ceramic dolls, filled with the books that you had sold off. And here was the sofa that I would no longer sit on. The phrase "Home makeover!" appeared repeatedly. What hina*mama described as a home makeover were things such as moving the sofa slightly, changing the direction the dining table faced, reorganizing the books on the bookshelf according to the colour of the spines or in alphabetical order by author or rearranging the way the silverware and cooking utensils lay in the drawer. Every time she made a change, she would take a photo and upload it.

There were also photos that didn't involve shuffling things around. She recorded changes in the light streaming in through the window, posting a series of shots taken at different times of day. Flowers, stems cut short, arranged in a jam jar. A drawer on a dresser, open halfway; inside it had been partitioned into a grid of equal squares, like a giant *go* board, and nested in each were different items— socks, or leggings, or nylons. A wide-open refrigerator, with the contents organized by containers and trays. A number of times, a wardrobe's worth of clothing spread out in an orderly fashion on the floor. hina*mama had a rule that every time she purchased new clothes, something old had to be got rid of. So there were also photos indicating what she had newly acquired and what she was going to let go. The same rule applied to children's clothes. Among the clothing that was featured, there were even a number of items that you yourself remembered seeing.

Together with the writers of the other blogs that you frequented, hina*mama was all about bringing order to everyday life, ruling it, restraining it. The pleasure that the women took in carrying this out is what captivated you. The joy it brought them was so immense, even you could see it. You became obsessed with these women. In your heart you felt an affinity with them, an understanding of them. You knew nothing about them, even whether they were alive or dead. But their desires were there for all to see. And hina*mama had the most straightforward desires of all, because she was dead and her desires were locked in place; they would never be changed or be deleted.

Your supposed "affinity" and "understanding" were, to be sure, self-determined; no one on the other side of the screen could vouch for whether these feelings were genuine, or how accurate they were. But you knew for yourself that you shared a feeling with these women and had an understanding of them that was deeper than anything you felt for the child right in front of you, or my father, or your parents and younger brother, or your friends and lovers, or even you yourself.

And in fact, you could no longer recall a single thing that had interested you before now, or that had made life worth living.

You thought back over your adult life. Over all of the days starting with when you went to college and lived on your own for the first time up until you came to live with my father in this apartment. You seemed to have survived all of that time without major incident. You had cooked, cleaned, done laundry, bought and thrown away things, thrown away and bought things, kept your wardrobe presentable, avoided major illness, done a passable job where you worked and earned your keep, and throughout all, had never known any pain or joy of note. You had nothing in particular that you wanted to write down and leave behind in this world, let alone anything that you hoped a large number of strangers would see someday.

It didn't occur to you that what these women were showing the world was a protective layer. What they most wanted was a physical and spiritual self that sparkled, free of flaws. They had painstakingly created the illusion of bodies and souls that existed as a collage of special-order goods.

You typed "umbellata" into the search engine window. You had seen this sequence of syllables any number of times on other blogs, and you'd correctly guessed that it had to be a houseplant.

Your dried-out eyes, tingling with pain, looked around at the living room. You did an image search for umbellata, raked through the mentions in the usual blogs and looked at umbellata for sale at online stores. There were many small umbellata that one could place in the corner of a desk, but what hina*mama wanted had to be one of the large variety that sit on the floor and stretch as wide as a person is tall. She must have hoped to place it next to the glass balcony doors and gaze at the sky through its mass of outsized, lush leaves. Maybe an umbellata would work well in the space between the pink curtains and the sofa. You decided you needed to buy one.

"We need a houseplant," you said to my father.

"Oh, that sounds great," my father agreed, without enquiring further. My father had no appreciation for plants, either.

You brought it up with the bookseller, who seemed like someone who would know more about them.

"I'm thinking about getting an... umbellata," you said.

"Oh, that would be a good one." As you had suspected, the bookseller knew his plants. "There's an umbellata in our cafe. I don't think they do anything special to take care of it, but it seems to be doing just fine." Because the bookseller had his lower lip pressed up against your shoulder, you heard his reply not as a voice in your ears but as a resonance thrumming through your body.

After you decided to purchase an umbellata, it still took a good three days to decide which site to purchase it from. There were all kinds of places that were selling them. Thousands of umbellata were ready to be shipped at the click of a button. Nearly every vendor included customer reviews—a lot of them. You read every one of them. That's what hina*mama would do, you thought. You didn't have time to meet up with your bookseller. Twice in a row, you called and cancelled on him.

"Why?" he asked you.

"Some stuff going on," you said.

"What kind of stuff?"

"I'm busy. All kinds of things."

You put your eye drops in. There was nothing to be done about the dry eyes your contact lenses gave you. You found yourself always putting in eye drops, and sometimes you had the feeling you were being watched.

"They're eye drops," you said, holding the little bottle out for me to see. I nodded.

Tears dripped down your face. I looked over at you again. My hand, which had been conveying snacks to my mouth, stopped in mid-delivery. With a practised hand, you took a contact lens out of your eye and held it between your thumb and forefinger up to the light.

"This is a contact lens," you said, licking some mote out of it and replacing it in your eye. I was still looking at you.

"My eyes are terrible, so if I don't put these in I can't see very well," you explained.

The umbellata showed up. The rectangular cardboard box was taller than you were. You pushed it, sliding it across the floor until you got it into the living room. I tottered along behind you and the plant. I didn't seem to have noticed that I had crossed over into the living room. You used a box cutter to open the packaging, and after you removed the packing material, the branches and leaves that had been carefully wrapped up opened out to fill the space around them. I came close to touch those giant leaves. When I did that, for some reason you reached out and touched one of my chubby cheeks. You didn't know that you wanted to touch my cheek; you just did it. It was drier than you had expected, just a little rough. This was the first time you had ever touched me this way. My entire body stiffened.

"Umbellata," you said, stroking the leaves with the same hand you had used to touch my cheek. For a time we were silent, each of us stroking the leaves that were closest to us. Despite their thinness, they felt fluffy and soft. They weren't smooth, but they weren't rough, either. They were there to be touched by us. It wasn't like touching a book; our fingers could stroke these leaves all day.

Eventually you got down on all fours and shoved the saucer underneath the pot inch by inch until the umbellata was between the curtains and the sofa. From your usual chair at the dining table, the green leaves seemed to rise up and over the armrest of the sofa, tumbling over one another. I was still standing in the middle of the living room. You let me be. A few moments later, I abruptly ran from the living room and got into the seat across from you.

My father could not for the life of him remember the word "umbellata". I needed to hear it only once before it was stuck in my mind. As you repeated it to him over and over—*umbellata umbellata umbellata*—I passed the time quietly burrowing my teeth between my fingernails and the skin underneath.

When I was at preschool, you opened the curtains, just about the first time you had done this since moving in. It was a rare sunny day in the middle of the rainy season. The light that poured into the living room overwhelmed you. You had to squint. The little scratches on your contact lenses caused the light to splinter across your field of vision. You stood still until your eyes adjusted—at least to the point that it wasn't painful—then got your mobile phone and took a photo of the umbellata. Our apartment was on the third floor; you didn't notice that the balconies of the adjacent apartment building were in the shot.

You sent the photo to your bookseller.

WHEN CAN I SEE YOU? was his response.

The moment those words flashed on the screen, the bookseller became a burden to you. It was very similar to the feeling you had had about your job the moment my father proposed living together. You sat down on the edge of the sofa and slouched back until you were practically staring at the ceiling.

I STILL DON'T KNOW, you started, then deleted it. You tried, NEVER, to see how it looked. You stared at that for a while, then deleted it too. It wasn't your style to say something like that.

I'M NOT SO SURE I WANT TO KEEP DOING THIS. That seemed about right. But then you didn't send it. In the end, you deleted it and sent no reply at all. This was your usual method of breaking up with someone.

From where you sat on the sofa, you sluggishly gazed at the Scandinavian cups and saucers you had decorated the bookshelf with. Bathed in the light streaming in, they took on a new beauty. The white of the ceramic had a silky shine, as though it might melt into air. You got to your feet and took a cup and saucer from the shelf. A thin layer of dust had collected at the bottom of the cup, since, after all, it was being used as a decoration and not as a cup. The dust gave off a faint gleam of its own. You rinsed the cup out in the sink and made some tea using a teabag. Then, for lack of anything better to do, you grabbed the novel that was standing alongside the cookbooks on the bottom of the bookshelf.

You plopped down at the end of the sofa, close to the umbellata, and studied the cover. The drawing of the prairie at night looked plain to your eyes, no charm, no style. But something about the vast emptiness of the scene that you held in your hands called out to you. For a while you stared at the night sky that had simply been painted a solid black.

As you had done before, you gently flipped through the pages of the book with your thumb. Once again, the pages created a little breeze that you felt in your eyes. You flipped through the book two or three times, and noticed that one of the pages was dog-eared at the top. The part folded over was so small that it was impossible to say whether someone had done it intentionally or whether it had just happened through use. You opened the book to that page, and read the line of dialogue that happened to be at the top:

"You need to try closing your eyes to all of it, too. It's just that easy. No matter how awful something is, it all goes away once you do that. If I can't see it, it's as if it's not even there. Not for me, anyway, it's not."

You sipped some tea, too much, and a hot numbness spread across your tongue. The passage you had just read seemed to flicker. It was as though the words on the page were smiling at you, greeting you like an old friend with a quick wave of the hand. You read the passage again, more carefully this time. Then you opened the book at random a few more times, each time reading the words on the page to see if the same thing would happen. It didn't. The pages seemed like a long line of people that you were looking down on from somewhere up on high, but you couldn't find any other bit of the text that would raise its chin to look up at you and give you a sign.

You put the book under your arm and turned on the television. The spectral colours of the screen began to flicker across the surface of your eyes. You smiled faintly. It looked as though you were laughing at something on the TV. But that's not really what was happening. You were trying to think about something. But about what you couldn't say, so there was no way to begin thinking about it. A clot of something that didn't lend itself to language was pressing down on your brain.

You never touched the book again, so you wouldn't have any way of knowing this, but the novel was a fantasy about an imaginary country ruled by a dictator. The lines that you found—the lines that found you—were the advice that the newly crowned despot whispered into the ear of his chosen biographer.

Your mobile phone chimed with an incoming text. Here was an excuse to stop trying to begin thinking about something. It could be argued that you had lost an opportunity to set your mind to work, but you didn't have any sense of that. To you, it felt as though your brain had been frozen and now rebooted. You picked up your phone. The text was from your bookseller. He had listed all the dates and times he was free to meet during the next two weeks. You closed the conversation and the curtains. It was time to pick me up.

By the following day, you had very nearly erased the book from your memory. And you didn't think about the bookseller, either. You had something else that you needed to do.

You began a thorough investigation of "Crystal-Clear Days". The photos that appeared on your laptop screen were of the size of the palm of your hand, small enough to strain your eyes even with your contacts in, but you searched every corner of the images for ideas. You threw out what was left of a jar of jam, washed the jar, and, just as hina*mama had done, arranged a spray of white chrysanthemums in it. You had gone to the flower shop without any idea what the flowers in the photo were called—you found them based on the colour and shape. You bought a linen blouse that was the same as one hina*mama had bought. Here again, you only had a photo to go on, so it took hours glued to your computer screen to figure out where she had bought it. You stopped buying white bread at the supermarket, and started going to the bakery to buy the whole-wheat bread that hina*mama had liked. Using the same white dishware that hina*mama had used, you served up the same herb-and-tomato salad that hina*mama had served up. You couldn't match hina*mama for presentation, but you weren't a very meticulous person in general, so this slipped by you.

My father was utterly oblivious to all of this. He had never really paid that much attention to my mother, and, when it came down to it, every last one of the things that my mother surrounded herself with and felt represented her individual sense of style was really just an ordinary item that anyone could get their hands on if they wanted it. The unbleached blouses, the navy-blue dresses, the T-shirts with the French Tricolore stripes, the French-made canvas trainers, the spray of chrysanthemums and baby's breath and turban buttercups, the whole-wheat bread, the brown rice, the salads that made liberal use of herbs, the chickpea and cauliflower soup—all of it, ultimately, was nothing special, and could be found everywhere.

You were a slave to petty pleasure. As always, the only joy you felt was in the acquiring; the hard-won furnishings were prized only as items for the collection. You were utterly powerless to stop yourself.

The umbellata began to wilt. I noticed it was happening before you ever did. As always, I spent my time chewing, on either snacks or my fingernails. The umbellata's foliage was never again as lush as the day it was delivered. In just a week, it waned to the point that even you noticed. The leaves dried out, turned yellow and shrivelled, dropping onto the floor. It was from a lack of sunshine. Day after day, you flooded it with water, which only made it weaker. You were regretful to the barest degree. You had no further use for the umbellata. There were so many other things you needed to get your hands on. The leaves that remained on the plant drooped, looking ever more pitiful, and in the end you sent the plant into exile on the balcony. When I returned home from preschool, nothing remained between the sofa and the pink curtains. Because the curtains had been closed for my benefit, I couldn't see that the umbellata was outside now. I became all the more engrossed with eating my snacks.

When the bookseller showed up at the apartment, you thought it was a delivery of one of the things you had ordered online. I was back from preschool, drinking milk and eating rice crackers at the table. Because new things were being delivered all the time, you and I had both got used to the intercom buzzing. I paid no attention to it. My brain echoed with the deafening sounds of rice-cracker crunching and milk guzzling. You got up to see who it was.

There was no response when you spoke through the intercom. You pressed the button over and over until finally a voice called out—from directly outside our door. Your bookseller had slipped in through the locked entrance to the building when someone else was entering or leaving.

"Whoa, what? What's going on?" you asked him. You had been ignoring the bookseller's texts for a full month at this point. Even when a man did something egregious like this, you couldn't bring yourself to use a cold tone of voice with him. "I mean. . . I'm sorry, but. . . when you suddenly show up like this. . . What should we do here? Wait just a bit," you said. There was laughter in your voice.

You looked back at me. With a smile on your face, you rushed up to me, grabbed onto the back of my chair and pulled on it, tilting it forward as you did so. The back legs of the chair came off the floor a little bit. I stood up. Part of the fabric of my trousers had been puckered up, catching all of my rice-cracker crumbs; as I stood, they scattered onto the floor. More bits of rice cracker were stuck to my fingertips, stained brown from the crackers' soy-sauce glaze. I was in the process of licking my fingers one by one. You put your hands on my shoulders and turned my body 180 degrees, so that you and I were face to face with one another. You pushed gently on both my shoulders, and I stepped backward from the pressure. You moved exactly that far forward to close the gap and keep on pushing. You were smiling the whole time. Even when I stumbled, you were unrelenting. Before I knew what was happening, you had pushed me all the way into the pink curtain.

I was still sucking on my fingers. They had been slathered with soy sauce, and the taste was just beginning to fade. Reaching over my shoulders, you groped through the curtains and opened the latch to the sliding glass doors. You nimbly slid open the door and gave my shoulders one last nudge. A blast of humid air clung to my skin. I looked up at you, and for the first time, I showed a sign of resistance. I stuck my left leg out behind me and planted my bare foot to brace myself, but it landed beyond the threshold of the balcony. You leaned down and lifted up my right foot, still on the floor inside the apartment, by the ankle, then released it. I would have fallen over backwards, if not for the umbellata. Its broad leaves caught me at my temples and elbows. The umbellata had revived. The leaves seemed to sway like a human's hair or clothing. Even though the skies were covered with thick, murky grey clouds, everything seemed unnaturally bright. The concrete balcony that I stepped out on was warmer than the soles of my bare feet.

"It's just for a little bit. A little bit. Give me five minutes. Sorry about this," you said. You rolled the sliding door shut, locked it and closed the curtain.

You ran your fingers through your hair as you went back to the entryway. You let your bookseller into the apartment. He kicked off his shoes and walked past you with long strides into the living room.

"I only have five minutes. I just put the girl out on the balcony," you said.

"Why don't you answer any of my texts?" the bookseller asked straight out. But he didn't seem upset. It was more as though he couldn't stand the strangeness of it any more.

"I've been busy, um. . ." you replied.

There was a sudden *whomp*. It registered not as a sound, but as a vibration that seemed to rumble through the wallpaper. You didn't look behind you. The bookseller looked past your eyes, over your head, to the pink curtains directly behind you. Another *whomp* shook the room. And then another. It didn't appear they would be stopping anytime soon.

"Tomorrow," the bookseller said quickly, his eyes darting back and forth between the curtains and your eyes. "Tomorrow, after you drop her off at preschool, come over and. . ."

The bookseller tried to caress your upper arm. You pulled away.

"If you don't want to meet again after that, fine, but come over tomorrow and we'll talk without the distraction."

The bookseller's face was more the colour of a slab of meat than of human flesh. The sides of his face were dry, and here and there the skin seemed to be peeling. You realized in this moment that your bookseller was a lot older than you.

You squeezed your eyelids shut tight, trying to get some moisture to your contact lenses. As you opened them, your contacts rode up your eyeballs slightly, pulled by the lids, before sliding down and fixing themselves in the right position. You nodded. The whole time, the *whomp*ing hadn't let up. The bookseller gave two curt little nods and left, looking over his shoulder at you as he headed out. You shut the door and ran your fingers through your hair again.

Even during the time it took you to open up the curtains and unlock the sliding door, I continued to pound with both of my fists on the glass. Because I was shaking the entire frame, it took you a few tries to get the lever unlocked. When you finally slid the panel open, I let out a strangled shriek and lunged at you. When I needed to, I had all kinds of words I could speak fairly clearly—I could have a proper conversation—but it was all a jumble this time. All I had were cheeks glimmering with tears and a primal growl.

You understood the language that poured out. You understood immediately the meaning of the words that I myself did not. You grabbed hold of my forearms and held me in place. How satisfying it was for you when your velvety fingers sank into my juicy forearms.

"OK," you said, and then put what you had read into your own words. "OK, look, I'm going to teach you something good. It's good to try not to see things. You should try it. It's good to just close your eyes to things. You can do it, so just, go ahead and try it."

I never forgot what you said. Years later, I found the book that had belonged to my mother, and, turning its old pages, listened to the words of the despot. I read the book from beginning to end. The despot behaved however he pleased, like a spoiled teenaged girl, and killed so many people he lost count. He killed more people than there were words in the book. A lot more. One couldn't say that the despot was perfectly happy, but he wasn't unhappy, either. At last there was a *coup d'état* and he was thrown into prison. Even when all he had to look forward to was his own execution, here again, he wasn't exactly happy about things, but you couldn't call him unhappy, either. His attitude during visits from his biographer was the same as it had always been. The despot prided himself on his ability not to see things. He was able through sheer force of will to turn a blind eye to the evils that he had committed. He squeezed his eyes shut and the sufferings of the flesh and spirit disappeared. For you and me, this was not an option. When it comes down to it, we are the powerless riff-raff.

Even *more* years later, when my arms had stretched out into slender length and I had lost all of that fatty meat practically dripping off the bone, replaced by what felt like a solid yet supple core; when wrinkles and redness had appeared in the joints of your fingers and the trace of your bones was visible through the skin on the back of your hands; when you no longer needed to look down to look me in the face; as you gripped my forearms and stared up at me, I repeated back to you those words I had committed to memory.

But all of that was still far in the future. With your hands pinching into my preschooler arms, I gnashed my teeth and breathed raggedly through my nose.

"You're fine," you said.

Before long, my arms and legs went numb and I lost the ability to stand. I was hyperventilating and had passed out. You grabbed me under my arms to keep me from falling, and carried me to the sofa and left me there. I conked out until the following morning. That evening, after dinner, my father lifted me up from the sofa and carried me to my bed. My father didn't sense anything strange about the fact that I was sleeping. It was strange that I was sleeping so long, but my father was actually pleased that I had been brave enough to go up on the sofa, so close to the sliding doors to the balcony.

The next morning I woke up as I always did, and prepared to go to preschool as I always did. I wouldn't look at you or talk to you. There was nothing new about this, but my face was much stiffer than usual, and I bit my nails the entire time we were walking to the school. You didn't try to stop me. I was carrying on with our ordinary lives without any crying or fussing, so you had no reason to complain about me.

You kept your promise to your bookseller. You went over to his apartment and said, "This is the last time." He swept his jumble of clothes off the bed and laid you down on it.

Afterward, you dozed off for a little bit. It was a shallow sleep, so shallow that you couldn't forget the sensation of the contact lenses in your eyes. You opened your eyes a slit, then closed them again; next to you, the bookseller lifted himself up. He looked down at you for a while, and then you sensed his face directly above your own.

He licked open your right eyelid, then expertly tongued your contact lens right off your eye. It hurt just to have your eye licked open, so it took you a few seconds to realize what else had just been done to you. You opened both eyes and looked directly up at him, but you couldn't figure out which eye was seeing everything clearly and which eye was registering everything as a murky haze. The bookseller's face didn't resolve as a single, clearly defined image. Its blurry contours wouldn't come into focus; everything oozed like an oily liquid.

You tried to sit up. The bookseller pushed down hard on your shoulders to prevent you from moving. His right hand clamped down on your forehead, holding it in place. You closed your eyes instinctively, but his thumb wormed its way down and pried open the lid of your left eye, which flooded from the pain. The bookseller licked up the lens together with your tears. He wasn't as smooth about it as he had been with your right eye. His tongue pressed down hard on your eye, causing tears to pour down your face.

Since you couldn't see anything clearly now, the bookseller went around and picked up your discarded clothing, handing things to you in the order in which you put them on.

"Why are you doing this?" you asked him. "You know I have to pick up the girl from preschool."

As his final gesture, your bookseller held out a box of tissues to you. You blew your nose, and wiped your eyes.

"Sorry," he said. In the entryway, he crouched down and pulled your shoes closer to the edge so that you could step down into them.

For the first time since elementary school, you were outside walking around without contact lenses or glasses. The sunlight was white, and the asphalt was black. Tears were brimming in your eyes. Your eyes ached. You wondered if this could be a dream. The swelling around your eyes, the bright light of the afternoon, the flow of strangers who came towards you or came up from behind and overtook you, the cars spewing their exhaust—none of it seemed real. It was like you had fallen through a wormhole into a certain distant memory.

Even the preschool, which should have been a familiar sight to you, didn't seem real. You bumbled forward, making your way among the voices of the preschoolers and the adults, moving like you were underwater. Even when an agitated voice called out to you, you didn't come out of your fog. When you turned towards where the voice came from, you saw—but not really—that someone was saying something sharp and rapid-fire in your direction. A group of women surrounded you now. They were followed by one of the teachers, who seemed to be trying to calm them down.

"What do you plan on doing if it leaves a permanent scar?" a woman asked sharply. In your mind, you pictured the fragments of your hard contact lenses working their way down the bookseller's throat.

"It was really close to her eye. If her eye got scratched like that, that's not the kind of thing that just heals," a different woman said. *Did all of that really happen back there,* you thought to yourself.

"Oh," you said. "Sorry."

Little by little, you came to understand what had happened: something made me snap and I had wounded several classmates.

"Sorry," you said again.

The teacher went into the office and called my name, motioning for me to come. You could tell that there were several children in there, knocking around in a cluster. One unsettlingly large blob abruptly separated from the writhing mass and stepped uncertainly towards you. There was no mistaking me, contacts or no contacts. I was roly-poly with cheeks to match, and I was bursting out of the clothes that no longer fit me.

"Hina has chewed her nails into jagged edges, and she suddenly started scratching the other students with them," the teacher reported to you. "This is something a mother has to pay attention to. You need to file down Hina's nails evenly."

"Oh," you said. "Sorry."

"Hina won't apologize. It's not like her at all, really. Did something happen, Hina?"

"Sorry," you said. "What do you say?"

I said nothing.

On our way home, you said, "I lost my contact lenses. I can't see very well. So you're going to have to help me." You took my hand and gripped it tightly.

"Yow," you said, dropping my hand right away. You crouched down next to me and clamped onto my fingertips. You held them close to your eyes so you could see them. My nails were so close to your eyes, so close.

"They're right. These are like little saws."

Until then, you had never once walked hand in hand with me, so you had never noticed.

You headed to the drugstore, where you bought some clear nail polish and a nail file. By the time you got back to the apartment you were exhausted; you felt you could fall asleep straight away.

But, before you slept, you put on your glasses and brought me to my chair at the dining table. I did as I was told; I didn't say a word, but I sat down and held out my hands. You sat down in your chair and then scraped it across the floor until it was next to mine. And then you filed my nails down one by one. When that was done, you blew on them and wiped them clean with a tissue.

"I'm going to paint your nails with polish, so you can't go biting them after this," you said to me in a calm voice.

You dabbed a blob of polish on each of my tiny nails and spread it evenly across the surface with a tiny brush. I looked at your glasses—they didn't flatter you—as you painted my nails, and the tension in my cheeks relaxed.

I sat there with a vacant look on my face, my head thrust forward, my back curled.

When you finished painting my last nail, you spread your fingers out in front of your face. "Now hold them like this until they're dry." I did as I was told. You stood up, had some tea and headed into your bedroom, leaving me where I was. When you came back out, having changed your clothes, my nails were almost dry. You checked this by dapping the tip of your finger across each nail, and then applied a second layer of polish. Once again I held my fingers spread in front of my face.

"Aren't they pretty? That's why you can't bite them." You took off your glasses and set them on the table. My nails really were beautiful. They gleamed, and there wasn't a single imperfection to be found.

You went over to the sofa and flopped down. Still sitting in my chair and holding my fingers out, I watched you stretch out. It wasn't unusual for you to lie on your back like that. But now, horizontal on the sofa, you looked like something the furniture store had thrown in as part of the package. You closed your eyes. But that's not to say that you fell asleep. You wanted to, but somehow you just couldn't drift off.

You were thinking about the thing that had happened when you were in high school. Four of you had got into an accident when the bicycle you were all on lost control flying down a steep road. In your memory the scene was incredibly bright, like overexposed film. It was startling to you how distant it seemed from your life now. To the adult you, the high-school you was far, far away. *A lot of water under the bridge since then*, you thought. But how young you still were to think such a thing. Sure, a fair amount of time had passed since high school, but in the grand scheme of things, not that much. You didn't have any sense of the fact that those days would continue to slide increasingly far into the past.

Your boyfriend at the time was the one with his feet on the pedals and his hands on the handlebars. He was a member of the rugby team. He was pedalling the bike almost standing up, so that you and another girl could occupy the seat, one squeezed in front of the other. The fourth member of the party was standing on the back cargo rack. She had her arms extended over you and the other girl and was holding on to your boyfriend's shoulders. This was the arrangement in which you were barrelling down a slope on a major road filled with large rumbling lorries. You held on to your boyfriend's waist, with the tip of your nose pressed firmly against his bum as it worked up and down, left and right, as he pedalled. The heat coming from the girl behind you, pressed right up against your back, was enough to start a wildfire. You were holding your legs out rigidly at an awkward level to keep them from scraping the ground, and everything had gone numb. But the thing you were most worried about was your contact lenses. You squeezed your eyes shut the whole time, to keep the wind from blowing them right out, so you had almost no idea what things looked like around you. The girl standing on the cargo rack was laughing wildly, screaming. Every time a lorry passed right next to the bicycle, the exhaust hit you full in the face. The sound of the engines drilled into your temples.

When the bicycle reached the bottom of the hill, your boyfriend couldn't get it to stop, and you all came crashing down in the road. The girl on the cargo rack broke her nose and chipped a front tooth. It would need to be replaced with an implant. The girl who was holding on to you had her right cheek and her right arm from the shoulder to the elbow sanded down by the asphalt. She didn't break any bones—all her injuries were scrapes—but the scrape was so deep in her right cheek that it left a mark on her face like a blue tattoo. After graduating from college, she underwent a series of laser treatments to gradually get rid of it. Your boyfriend sprained both of his wrists and suffered bad scrapes on his face, chest and stomach. The front of his jeans were shredded and his thighs were bloodied.

on you. You didn't pay it any heed. But soon, the presence was directly over your face.

Your right eye was wrenched open. And then a small warped disc, opaque like frosted glass, was pressed down into your eye. Pain ripped through you. The sting of the bookseller licking off your contact lenses was nothing compared to this. Your eyes pooled with tears, trying to flush the disc out. You tried to bring your hands to your eyes, but you couldn't. A rib-cracking heavy weight landed on your chest, and your elbows were locked in place. I had climbed up onto your chest, and my knees were pinning down your arms. I was so heavy I forced air out of your lungs; your vocal cords made a funny noise as your breath was forced past them. I laughed. I tugged at your left eye, forcing it open. I jammed another frosted, warped disc into the very centre of your eye. Your head jerked wildly back and forth, causing my finger-nails, which you had ever-so-gently and unintentionally sharpened, to slice across your cheeks, and forehead, and eyelids.

My deed done, I put my fingers and thumbs to both eyes and forced them open. Your tears would not stop gushing, but they couldn't wash away these pale discs. You thought that they had to be fish scales or something like that, but you were wrong. They were the layers of nail polish that my well-trained teeth had cleanly ripped off my thumbnails.

The lacquer just about covered your irises, leaving only a cloudy grey at the centre of your eyes. I bent forward, peering into your wide-open eyes as your tear ducts and sinuses overflowed. "Now can you see everything clearly?"

You didn't answer. You couldn't see anything that you could make sense of. There was only light. In front of you, there was brightness. And a surprising clarity. Your past and future, equally clear, stretched out from your body into the distance. You weren't able to focus on any single particular event. But all the time that had passed to this point in your life and all the time that remained to you had formed into a single plane of glass that now threatened to cut you in half at the waist.

I can see that sheet of glass coming ever so close to me now. My eyes have always been superior, so I was able to see it gleaming in the distance while it was still far away. The difference between you and me is that one minor thing. Other than that, there is no daylight between us.

WHAT
SHOKO
FORGETS

S omeone new is in the room, gently breathing. There are four beds, so there should be four patients, but now, there is one other person here, inhaling, exhaling.

"Shoko."

A voice is whispering to her, but Shoko keeps her eyes shut.

"Shoko."

The voice comes closer, close enough that she feels it on her eyelashes. Shoko scrunches up her eyelids to keep everything sealed extra tight.

A deep, restrained voice speaks to her. "Shoko, you always pretend you're asleep." He is enjoying this.

Always? Shoko thinks about this. Oh, that's right. Always.

Shoko remembers that they go through this every night. Why did she forget? She remembers now that, in fact, she forgets it every morning and remembers it every night. She remembers *that*, too. Every night, a man slips into this room for four people, and she is brought out of her light slumber by his gentle breathing.

Mornings, Shoko awakens with the feeling that she doesn't care for anything in this world. She doesn't like the hospital, or the hospital food, or the yolky-yellow walls, or the doctors and nurses, or her own family. All of which is to say, Shoko doesn't like herself at all.

Half a year ago, Shoko had a mild stroke. Since then, she has been living in facilities. The general hospital released her in short order, and she was transferred to the rehabilitation centre. Her children decided that Shoko's oldest daughter would be the one to handle all arrangements, and she is the one who always comes to help. Sometimes Shoko's oldest daughter's oldest daughter comes, but it is scandalous how little this granddaughter of hers does to help. For the most part, she sits in a chair and laughs, while her mother busies herself with Shoko. "How are you doing, Grandma?" she says, a little too chipper. When food is brought in, she is all smiles: "Ooh, doesn't that look good?" She saves her biggest smile, a genuine one, for the young man, Kawabata. "Hello again, nice to see you."

Kawabata was admitted as a patient right after Shoko was transferred here. He must be in his early twenties, although he looks like a teenager. In a wing that is full of people who are middle-aged or elderly, he is by far the youngest. He is tall and lanky, and gets around perfectly well.

"Young people recover so quickly. How nice that he can get around by himself and handle his own rehabilitation," Shoko's daughter mused.

Kawabata is forever wandering the halls, poking his head into the lounge, and charging up and down the stairs. Only when he happens upon someone with whom he can ride the lift does he not take the stairs. Kawabata doesn't have a shy bone in his body. Every single time he passes a patient in the hall, man or woman, he greets them, starts up a conversation and is quick to lend a hand. And not just the patients. He sometimes jumps up to carry heavy things for weighed-down visitors, and if the visitors are old, he slows his pace to match theirs, just as he does with other patients, and makes a point of enunciating his words more than usual. Kawabata is undergoing physical therapy, so no one doubts his need to stay in the centre, but when he so easily performs every task the therapists give him, a newcomer could be forgiven for wondering what exactly is wrong with him.

Kawabata is, generally speaking, a beloved figure here, and he is the only person Shoko likes in the whole place. He shows far more sympathy for Shoko than does her own daughter, or granddaughter, or any of the nurses. And that is what Shoko wants most of all. Shoko is smaller and more frail than any of the other patients. She has broken a femur in the past, and her legs are bad. Her worn-down body was rickety even before she had the stroke. Kawabata seems to understand that she is infirm, that her body is crumbling. His sad smile seems to say, "They shouldn't be trying to make you do anything." When Shoko clutches her walker and stands up, Kawabata holds out his soft-looking hands and crouches down just a bit, as if steeling himself to support her on a second's notice.

Whenever a nurse or her daughter—sometimes both—accompanies Shoko to the bathroom, Kawabata appears out of the blue and goes with them as far as the door. He has been known to wait until she is done and then to accompany her back to her room. When Kawabata bends over so that he can talk to her at eye level, he is like a stem drooping under the weight of flowers in bloom. Shoko loves the organic curve of his body. Kawabata always wears T-shirts that are too long and shorts that end at his knees, making it appear that he has an absurdly long torso. But Shoko feels a closeness to that disproportionate body.

The other day, when Shoko was drinking some apple juice, when she just wanted to fill her stomach up with apple juice but her daughter said it would ruin her appetite for the nice food the facility had prepared and took away her cup when it was still half full, Kawabata waited until her daughter stepped away and slipped her another cupful.

"This is our little secret, Mrs Sasaki," he said with a smile. Kawabata calls her by her name. All the patients wear wristbands with their full names on them. Kawabata reads them and remembers them. Shoko likes that about him, too. Shoko never has much of an appetite, and that day she gladly left most of her meal on the tray. Her daughter was worried—maybe Shoko wanted something else? Should she get the rest of the apple juice out of the fridge, would Shoko like that? Shoko turned away from her.

Shoko simply does not like anything.

At night, the chilled apple juice in her stomach is heavy like rage. Shoko has lived for a long time, she has seen a lot in her day, and she should be at a point in her life where she sets down her burden and takes it easy. She doesn't understand why she is being prevented from eating what she wants when she wants, or why she needs to be in a facility where she really doesn't want to be. She has let everything go, so she doesn't understand why only her body remains—or when her body became the burden.

Shoko closes her eyes. She listens to the sound of four people breathing, including herself. Very soon, it comes to her, that number will increase. Very soon, she thinks, there will be five people in this room.

And sure enough.

"Shoko," the voice whispers, and Shoko remembers everything.

"Shoko."

His head quietly comes down near to hers. She doesn't need to open her eyes to know his movements. He gently takes her wrist, which is sticking out from beneath her bedcover. With his thumb, and then with his middle finger, he strokes the skin on the back of her hand. He strokes with the utmost care this skin which is luminous because of how thin it has become. He traces the veins that burrow just beneath the skin.

"Shoko."

Shoko holds her breath; she doesn't want to breathe in the lukewarm air that he is exhaling. He laughs without making a sound. She can feel the rhythm of it tapped out through his hands. Because Shoko remembers everything, she knows what he is going to do next—the sound of it, and the shaking. No, not from that stifled laugh of his. It is a more horrible sound and percussion that she braces herself for.

One of the residents of Shoko's room is discharged. The woman is much younger than Shoko, and fairly full-figured.

The woman changes into her regular clothes to leave the facility and sweeps the partition curtain open. As she wriggles her feet into her shoes, she makes her official announcement to Shoko. "I'm finally getting out of here." Behind her, a middle-aged woman who appears to be family is stuffing her things into a travel bag.

Shoko's daughter is not scheduled to be here today. When Shoko is finished with her exercises and returns to her room accompanied by the physical therapist, her roommate is gone. The woman's sheets and blankets are still on the next bed over. On the dresser is a vase of tulips that has been left behind. The petals have fallen, the stamens too, leaving only the wilting pistils.

Shoko is drifting in and out of consciousness. The rehabilitation centre has a limit on the number of days a patient can stay here. Once your allotment is up, you are released whether you want to be or not. Shoko knows this, but she is still plagued by the dread that she will never be able to leave here as long as she lives. Of course, this isn't a place people are sent to die. Shoko knows hospitals where people are sent to die. Nine years ago, Shoko's husband was diagnosed with cancer, and he died in one of those places. This place is nothing like that place. Shoko wants to go home as soon as she can. She wants to go home and, instead of all this tasteless hospital food, she wants to eat snacks, as much as she wants. And relax on the couch. And turn on her favourite TV shows and drift in and out of sleep for the rest of time.

Shoko opens her eyes. She is facing the unoccupied bed. Kawabata is sitting there. He is half-turned away from her, touching the tulip petals scattered around the vase.

Shoko watches him, wondering if she is still sleeping. She moves not a muscle, continuing to breathe as she did while asleep. The only thing that has changed is that her eyes are open, watching Kawabata's fingers, which are idly sifting through the tulip petals. There is a memory in there, Shoko thinks. Kawabata's thumb and middle finger stroke the surface of a petal. The petals haven't yet completely dried out; they are shrivelled and thin, but there is still enough moisture in them that they are a little soft. Without realizing she is doing it, Shoko caresses the back of one of her hands with the other.

Kawabata turns to face her. "Mrs Takemoto was released, wasn't she?" he says calmly. He looks down. Shoko is still stroking the back of her hand. Kawabata watches her doing it.

"I'll clean up the tulips," Kawabata says brightly. "I wonder if the vase belongs to the facility. I'll wash it and take it to the nurses' station."

He scoops up the tulip petals and curled-up stamens and drops them into the vase, which still has water in it. He picks up the vase and bows as he steps away from Shoko. At the doorway, he finds one of Shoko's roommates slowly making her way in from the hallway, leaning on a cane. Kawabata stops in his tracks and moves aside for her, crouching forward to match her height. His long torso bends to a shocking degree, with a crook in the centre of his back, somewhere south of his shoulder blades. Shoko very nearly lets out a scream. Are human torsos meant to bend like that? Surely there is something wrong with him, she thinks.

Kawabata passes Shoko's bed again, guiding the other patient back to her own bed further from the door. The whole time he maintains that impossible posture, with only his head turned up to face forward and a hand extended to the patient's back, riding the fine line between touching and not touching. Kawabata has his usual melancholic smile. Shoko's eyesight has grown truly terrible, but she can still see one thing: Kawabata's expression. *You shouldn't have to walk any more. There's no point in forcing you to walk when it's so difficult for you.*

"I thank you, I thank you," the patient says to Kawabata in a loud voice.

At night, the breathing of three people becomes the breathing of four. "Shoko," the voice calls out to her. Why am I going to forget all about this by morning? Shoko wonders. Maybe because if she were to open her eyes, she wouldn't see him there. Even if she did open her eyes, the lights are off—there's no way she could see him in the darkness. Shoko squeezes her eyes shut all the more.

He presses his lips to the scrunched-up corners of Shoko's eyes.

A new patient moves into the neighbouring bed. A relative of the new person and Shoko's daughter are conversing in hushed tones.

"Honestly, hospitals are all but rolling the patients out the front door to get them out. And no one is allowed to stay *here* very long, either."

"They go home and they get weak again and then they're right back where they started. It just seems like old people get all this physical therapy work here, but then the moment that they get to where they are supposedly able to maintain things on their own. . ."

The partition curtain rolls back, and her daughter comes in. "Mum, let's be sure to meet your new neighbour later on," she says, as she briskly folds some towels and Shoko's underwear.

"Where is Mr Kawabata's injury?" Shoko asks out of the blue, her voice hoarse.

"Huh, Kawabata? Well. . . oh, speaking of which, Kawabata was in the lift just now."

"Why is he still here in the rehabilitation centre?" Shoko's tone is much sharper now. It almost sounds as though she is blaming her daughter.

"I would have no idea. But something must be wrong with him if he's here, right?"

"Does he look to you like he needs to be here?"

"Well, Mum, that's the kind of thing you can't really ask. . . I don't think we need a detective on the case."

In the afternoon, her granddaughter comes as well. As always, she does nothing to help—just pulls out a chair and sits there grinning dumbly. She doesn't look like she could be trusted with anything, but her presence seems to give her mother a boost; Shoko's daughter's colour is better, she seems to have more get-up-and-go. But Shoko's daughter is far too indulgent with this girl who isn't married yet. Shoko's granddaughter is facing this way and looking directly at Shoko, but the whole time she is talking to her mother, who is standing behind her.

"... hey, um, that Kawabata, um," her granddaughter is saying cheerily, "he said, 'Hey, you cut your hair.' All I did was give myself some fringe. To a woman, fringes are a big deal, right? But it's totally shocking how boys don't notice things like that. But then here comes Kawabata with this serious expression on his face, and he goes, 'They really frame your face nicely.' He may be young, but he really thinks about other people, that guy."

Shoko looks up at her granddaughter. Her chest tightens just thinking about her. How old is this girl? How old is this girl sitting here dressed like she's in junior high with her jeans and T-shirt?

Shoko asks her granddaughter how old she is.

"Huh? I'm thirty-seven, Grandma," she says without a trace of shame. "I'm getting to be an old lady." You would think she couldn't smile more than she normally does, but she manages to.

"I get the shivers just thinking about it," Shoko's daughter says, smiling in a somewhat more sane way.

Thirty-seven! Shoko is astounded. When she was thirty-seven, she already had children. A pile of children, and plenty of them boys, so many that no one in her family or in the neighbourhood would ever have reason to criticize. At thirty-seven, Shoko had already put sex behind her.

That passing thought kind of riles Shoko up. Why does she have to go thinking about sex at this point in her life? Sex is one of those things that she is well and truly done with, a burden that no one in their right mind could possibly expect her to bear at this point in her life. But this granddaughter of hers hasn't let it go yet. Or maybe she has, secretly?

The silk-screen design on Shoko's granddaughter's T-shirt is warped out of shape by her breasts. Her thick fringe is cut straight across, earrings dangle from her ears, and she has this muck around her eyes for make-up—all of this only to traipse around in jeans and a T-shirt.

Her granddaughter stands up. "I should get going, Grandma. I have to get to work."

Shoko's daughter trails her out of the room, saying, "Be careful, hon. What are you doing for dinner? Are you coming home to eat?"

"What is that girl doing with her life?" Shoko grumbles when her daughter comes back into the room.

"Mum, we've been over this. You know that she's a writer, right? Remember? A freelance writer?"

"I mean, is she ever going to get married?"

Her daughter seems relieved by this. "Well, I'm sure she will at some point. But, you know, she's pretty busy."

Her daughter says this flippantly, as though she isn't worried about it in the least.

At night, until the fifth presence comes into the room after lights out, Shoko nods off and thinks about sex without even realizing it. And when she realizes that she has been thinking about sex, she isn't happy about it. There are all kinds of other things she wants to think about, that she should be thinking about. One would think sex is in that category of things she will never encounter again.

And yet, she can't banish it from her mind.

It has been about half a century since the last time she had sex. The occasion was not recorded in her memory as having been anything special.

One particular act of sex blends into the next, blurring together with the sex she had at yet another time, such that any individual act is lost to memory. She no longer remembers how it would start or how it would end, or when the first time was or when the last time was. For Shoko, "sex" is a murky mix of all the times she ever had sex, covering—like a thin layer of dust—a span of a few years that are located roughly half a century in the past.

The breathing of this fifth person in the room is churning up that dust.

"Shoko," he calls out to her. "Shoko, I'm here."

Oh, boy, Shoko thinks, squeezing her eyes shut.

He climbs into Shoko's bed with a practised movement. Shoko's frame is so tiny that there is plenty of space in her bed. He lies down next to Shoko.

He pulls himself snug against her and turns onto his side, looking at her from such close range that his eyes can't focus on her. Shoko can sense this. Even though there cannot possibly be enough light in this dark room for him to see anything, his eyes are open wide and staring at her, not blinking. Under this intense gaze, the fuzz on Shoko's cheeks stirs.

Shoko is sitting on a bench in the rehabilitation room. Her daughter is some distance removed, asking questions of the physical therapist and taking notes. The therapist glances at what her daughter has written down, points to the notepad and explains a little more. Her daughter nods. Her daughter dyes her hair black, and at the part it glistens white.

"Hello, Mrs Sasaki." Kawabata comes into the rehabilitation room and sits down next to Shoko. As always, he is wearing an overlong T-shirt.

"Getting fixed up? Did you finish your session already? I bet you're beat," Kawabata says consolingly. Shoko looks up at his smiling face. *You shouldn't have to do this rehabilitation. What does it matter if you can't stand on your own?* Come to think of it, she really is tired. Every part of her feels heavy, and she feels as if she really can't stand up. Shoko hangs her head as though she is truly exhausted.

When she does so, she finds herself looking at Kawabata's reddish-brown bare legs, sticking out of his knee-length shorts. His legs are lean and tight, with black hairs sprouting up and wriggling around, like new buds from the earth. Shoko feels her bones, riddled by osteoporosis, fill with revulsion. Shoko raises her head in a huff and scoots forward with her hips until she is teetering at the edge of the bench, scowling at Kawabata the entire time. Kawabata, alarmed, spreads his giant hands to support her. Although they are twiggy with knots for joints, the pads of his fingers and the base of his thumbs are plump, and the lines in his palms glisten with sweat. Shoko brushes him back with a wave of her arm, which is draped with thinning skin.

"You stay away from my daughter. And my granddaughter, too," Shoko says.

Shoko stands by herself. She's a little unsteady with

these hips, but if she has a mind to do it, she can stand up any time she damn well pleases. Her daughter notices and comes jogging over.

"Mum, what's wrong? Are you tired of waiting? Do you want to go back to your room?"

Shoko says nothing, but digs her fingers into her daughter's arm and turns towards the door of the rehabilitation room. Her daughter stiffens her arm to brace for the possibility Shoko will put all her weight on it. She pulls the walker that is off to her side over in front of Shoko, but Shoko stubbornly refuses to let go of her daughter's arm. Her daughter gives in and moves together with Shoko out into the hallway, as the physical therapist pushes the walker alongside them. Shoko's daughter glances back and gives Kawabata a slight bow. Kawabata, a perplexed smile on his face, watches the threesome move away.

"Mum, what is going on?" her daughter asks again, keeping her voice low. But Shoko doesn't have an explanation for her.

"That kid gives me the creeps," she finally mumbles. "He's a little too familiar in the way he talks to total strangers."

Her daughter tries to soothe her. "Mum, Kawabata just has too much time on his hands. Don't you think he's a kind, nice young man?"

Now more than ever, Shoko despises anything and everything: Kawabata, and her daughter who doesn't understand a thing, and her granddaughter who acts like a child well into her adulthood, and herself: an old woman who forgets her own name until the moment someone calls her by it.

Shoko's name is not Shoko.

That night, when the man lying beside her whispers, "Shoko," Shoko comes very close to blurting that out to him. *My name is not Shoko. You got that by reading the characters on my wristband, right? You could pronounce them "Shoko", but that's not how they're pronounced in my name.*

Instead, though, Shoko continues to pretend she is sleeping. She isn't going to engage with him. Far better for him to go on using the wrong name forever.

The man lolls on his side and stares at her point blank, his chest pressed up against Shoko's shoulders. The first thing she hears is a sound. The sound of a beating heart.

There is no longer a single cloud in the sky of her consciousness; she is completely lucid. She knows that she couldn't fall asleep even if she tried to. The sound of his heartbeat echoes through her body, not just through her body but through the entire room, so utterly, utterly loud that sleep is out of the question.

Not to mention the shaking. His heart thumps, pulsating through the expanse of his chest, which is pressed up against Shoko's shoulders so tightly that the percussion begins to pound into them. But before long, her shoulders alone cannot tamp it down. Shoko's entire body begins to wobble. *Stop it, enough with the shaking. Get that beating heart away from me,* she pleads, but he never listens. Now her entire body is convulsing on top of the bed, bouncing like a rag doll. Shoko's front four teeth, top and bottom, are dentures, which she removes every night, but to make sure she doesn't bite through her tongue with her back implants, she grinds them together.

She knows from all of the previous nights that there is no use crying out. For starters, even though Shoko's body is bouncing up and down on the bed, her three roommates seem blissfully unaware of it, each of them far away in her own slumber. Even if Shoko were to cry out, there would be little hope of anyone awakening. They will wake up only when they are good and ready to.

And so, Shoko stays stone silent, her body thrashing up and down on the bed. If this keeps up, it's going to dislocate her delicate shoulders and hips. With her eyes still closed, she chooses her moment and out of desperation pulls her knees up. Shoko curls up into a ball, grabs hold of her folded legs and presses her mouth up against her kneecaps. Actually, ever since she broke her femur, she hasn't been able to get into this position. But now her muscles are pliant, stretching and bending into place. Her sorry sags transform into solid sinew, and her entire body becomes a living heart. As a woman, Shoko is extremely petite, but as a heart, she is wondrously large. Shoko no longer has the power to think now that she has turned into a heart. All of her energy is poured into the pulse. Not of his heartbeat, but rather, of the thumping heartbeat that is Shoko. She beats all by herself, now. She is alive, not as a sentient being called Shoko, but as pure throb.

"It's all going to be all right, Shoko," he says, holding her in a tight embrace. He holds tight to this giant heart pulsing so violently that it threatens to break apart. Until the dawn, he holds it tight.

MINUTE
FEARS

There was so much curry it was threatening to spill out of the pot. I washed the pan and strainer, cleaned up and looked at the clock on the wall. 3:50. Daiki was surely at the pocket playground. That's where he was whenever he had the chance, stopping by on his way home from school or, like today, going over on a Saturday when the weather was nice. I set the rice cooker so that it would be done by 7:00, took off my apron and headed to the bathroom. I scrubbed the tub and the tile floor. Exactly 4:00. I sat down at the kitchen table and started applying nail polish to my fingernails. The polish was a dull gold; I'd bought it at the convenience store—395 yen—expressly for today. Was Daiki bouncing on one of those half-buried tyres, launching himself off it like it was a vault? Or going down the line of tyres, hopping from one to the next? If not, then he had to be monkeying around on the climbing frame. I couldn't imagine anything else he could be doing there, because, really, those were the only things to do in the cramped little park. And although the climbing frame was globe-shaped, it didn't revolve, which is what makes something like that fun in the first place.

But everyone in Daiki's class was under the spell of their pocket playground. Or so Daiki said. I spread the fingers of my hands out and held them over the table. Because my nails are so short, my hands looked more childlike now than they did when I didn't have any polish on them. I should have just used some press-on nails, I thought. But no need to get obsessive about little things. I brought all of my make-up out from the bedroom and propped up a folding mirror the size of a small paperback on the kitchen table. I plucked my eyebrows with the tweezers. Then I squeezed some liquid foundation out onto my fingertips and set to work. 4:18.

We had received a message from the school requesting that students bring a large tin to art class. Any kind of tin was fine, lid not needed, because it would be used for a papier-mâché diorama on the theme of "My Favourite Place". I tried to give Daiki a rectangular biscuit tin, but he wasn't having it. "I don't want something long like this—it has to be square!" he said firmly. When I asked him why, he said it was because the pocket playground was square.

At that point, I hadn't seen the pocket playground with my own eyes. According to Daiki, it was halfway between the elementary school and our apartment building. It seemed strange that I had never seen it if it was so close to us, but Daiki explained that it didn't face the street. "There's a store that has pink and yellow stripes on the shutters," Daiki said. "The park is behind it. Next to the store is an old, run-down house, and there's a path between them. That's how you get to the park." I remembered the shop with the shutters—it was a bedding store that had gone out of business. It was in a building with other businesses above it, but after the bedding shop vacated, nothing came along to take its place at street level. I could picture the traditional wooden house next to it. I didn't remember the path between the two buildings, but when I passed by a few days later, sure enough, there it was. The path was narrow, less than a metre across. The roof of the house jutted out over it and blocked out the sun, so it was dark. It seemed to be paved with asphalt, like the pavement I was standing on, but the pavement was greyish brown, and the path was black, like scorched earth.

After filling in my eyebrows a bit darker than usual, I curled my eyelashes and applied mascara. Painstakingly I applied it to my lower lashes as well. Some lashes clumped together—probably because the mascara was old. With a toothpick, I delicately separated each lash. I unclipped the hair-slide at the back of my neck, freeing my hair. It bounced back, showing no sign of having been bound up.

Daiki ended up taking a bright red Milky milk-sweets tin to school for his art project. He complained bitterly that this was something a girl would choose, but I couldn't find anything else at the neighbourhood supermarket that would work. A few days later, Daiki returned from school carrying the miniature landscape he had created. It was rare for him to come directly home, but he wanted to show it to me before anything fell apart. He held the red tin out to me, cradling his masterpiece. And that was how I got my first glimpse of the pocket playground.

In the middle of the park, on brown ground, was a misshapen sphere of twisted strands of papier mâché that had been glued together in a grid pattern. The papier mâché was unpainted, with Daiki's fingerprints visible everywhere. Circling the sphere were thirteen caterpillars, arching their backs in the air. The caterpillars looked sick. Their red, green, sky blue and purple bodies were speckled yellow and had black stripes. In the corner stood a man painted completely white. His head was flat and drooping forward, his body nothing but a long, narrow post. When I held the tin up at eye level, I peered at the face of the little man; he had a frown that Daiki had drawn in pencil, one side drooping further down than the other.

"It's the clock," Daiki said.

Speaking of which, 4:45. I finished doing my make-up and stuffed everything back into its case. I had to leave the house by 5:30 at the latest. I was going to a wedding reception for a friend from college. A cafe had been rented for the occasion, and we were all chipping in 6,000 yen. I had told Daiki that today he needed to be home by 5:00. From the pocket playground to our house, it was less than a five-minute dash, even for a seven-year-old. But knowing him, I was sure he was going to keep playing until as close to 5:00 as he could. It would be nice if right about now he started paying attention to that clock.

The clock kept good time. I knew this because I went to see the real pocket playground in person once. It was maybe a month after Daiki had brought home his tin diorama, late in the afternoon, about the same time as it was right now. The time on the clock was dead on.

That morning, Daiki had been lazing around in bed, not wanting to get up. *What's going on—get up, you're going to be late for school.* No matter how many times I called out to him, Daiki only groaned. He had nearly buried himself in his futon. But an entire arm was thrust out jauntily, its palm pressed up against the tin next to his head.

From the day he brought the diorama home, Daiki had been sleeping with it next to his pillow. The papier-mâché frame of the climbing frame had, as the days had gone by, crumbled at the edges and now was beginning to collapse. Every morning, pieces of the playground were scattered across the sheets. Daiki would pick the fragments up one by one and place them back into the tin. And that's how his project morphed from a little park to a scene of caterpillars feasting on the carcass of a small animal and gnawing it down to the bones.

This is a strange scene, I said with a laugh.

"It feels good because it's nice and cool," a muffled voice said from somewhere inside the duvet. That's how I realized that Daiki had a fever.

Towards evening, Daiki called out, "I want some ice cream," and I went down to the convenience store to get some. Along the way, as I was going past the abandoned bedding shop, a wave of children came pouring at full speed out from the path alongside it. Everyone was screaming at the top of their lungs. Some were laughing, while others were crying in terror. I recognized several of their faces. They were my son's classmates. They gathered in front of the closed store, gasping for breath. The screaming died down, the crying too, to be replaced by a clamour of voices counting: "One, two, three, four. . ." I watched all of this from the pavement on the other side of the street. The group chanted their way to ". . . sixty!" and then charged back up the dark, narrow path.

I crossed the street and followed where the children had disappeared down the path. There was a brightness at the end that seemed to glow. The pocket playground was a square parcel of land bordered on one side by the breeze-block wall behind the traditional wooden house, and on an adjacent side by the mixed-use building itself. The other two sides had chain-link fencing, beyond which was a large car park. So, there was nothing that blocked the light from the west; everything in the playground felt the glare of the afternoon sun.

The actual pocket playground was pretty much the way Daiki had depicted it in his diorama. A slightly dingy globe-shaped white climbing frame stood fixed in the middle of the space. Surrounding it were the half-tyres, painted in garish colours. The clock was there as well. The only piece that Daiki hadn't been able to work into his diorama was a blue bench along the wall of the building of the former bedding shop. The bench had split apart almost down the middle, and red tape with the words "Do Not Use" was strung across it. School backpacks lay on the ground where they had been flung with no regard for their contents.

The children were so engrossed in their play that no one turned to see me standing there. Most of them were on the climbing frame, scuttling across the bars in such a tight cluster that they looked like a single giant creature with its tentacles wrapped around the globe. Two or three children were bouncing from half-tyre to half-tyre, in perpetual motion around the climbing frame.

The intercom buzzed as I was zipping up my dress in back. I checked the clock. 4:50. I barely had time to think, Oh, it must be Daiki, home earlier than I thought he would be, when the buzzer started blaring in rapid-fire bursts. Abandoning my zip, I rushed to the door. Scanning the shoes lined up in the foyer, I stepped on a pair of rubber slippers that I thought would do the least damage to the bottom of my stockings and leaned forward to reach the doorknob. Daiki was calling out, "Mum! Mum! Open up!"

Without my hair-slide, my hair fell over my eyes as I opened the door. I couldn't see Daiki's face or much of anything, but I could see his school trainers. *OK, you don't need to yell to the entire neighbourhood,* I started to say, and the trainers jerked backward a step. I pulled my hair behind my ears and looked him in the eyes.

Daiki was expressionless. Or possibly angry. A second ago he had been shouting for me to open the door, but now his jaw was set and he was perfectly quiet. When his eyes met mine, he took another step back. The knees of his trousers were scuffed and dirty. *Oh, Daiki, what happened? Did you fall?* I bent down to dust them off, but he stood just out of reach. *Well, what did you do? Come closer*, I said, and Daiki at last responded with a grunt.

The moment he was through the door, Daiki kicked off his trainers and raced to the living room. I headed to the bathroom washbasin, washed my hands and returned to my battle with the zip. I managed to close it up to the top, and then after a valiant struggle even managed to fasten the clasp.

While I was brushing my hair, I thought about how I had to praise Daiki not just for keeping his word, but also for coming home a full ten minutes early. I gathered up my hair in back, twisted it up, and tried keeping it in place with a decorative comb. The comb had pearls embedded in it. Last year, when I was invited to a different friend's wedding, I bought it to go along with this dress. I also bought a bolero jacket with gold lamé threaded throughout it and T-strap pumps in a matching gold. But the day before the event, my husband was admitted to the hospital with what turned out to be appendicitis. And so, tonight would be the first time I wore the outfit out of the house.

The comb fell out, and my hair fell to my shoulders. I couldn't get the comb to stay in place no matter what I did. Right after I bought it, I had practised with it over and over, and got to the point where I could get it to hold all my hair together tightly. But now nothing I did was working, and my arms were going numb from holding them above my head for so long. And I was running out of time. I gave up and brushed my hair again. It wasn't so bad like this. I stood up straight and inspected myself in the bathroom mirror. My dress was dark green and made of polyester. It had all the lustre of silk with none of the wrinkling. Shortly after I graduated from college, I got pregnant and then got married. Of the female friends I was about to meet up with, some were married, but I was the only one with a child. But that didn't make me feel out of place. I was almost ten pounds lighter than I was in college, and I had stopped slathering on the make-up. Maybe that's why my skin was so healthy. My husband, sweetheart that he is, told me I looked younger than ever.

I turned away from the mirror, about to leave the bathroom, when I was startled—and gasped in surprise. The door to the cramped bathroom was slightly ajar, and there in the crack was Daiki's face looking up at me. He was crouching on the floor in the hallway, his arms wrapped in a death grip around his knees. I wondered how long he had been there staring at me. *What are you doing down there?* I asked him, my alarm turning to laughter. *You're going to give your mother a heart attack.* I rested my hand on Daiki's head as I eased past him and walked into the living room. Daiki crawled on all fours after me. 5:03. I gathered up everything I used to do my make-up from the kitchen table and hurried towards the bedroom. Daiki stood up and followed me. *What is it? You can watch TV in the living room,* I said, as I put on my engagement ring and my pearl earrings. I picked up the bolero from the bed where I had laid it out and slipped my arms through the sleeves, then picked up my handbag. Daiki stood immobile in the doorway to the bedroom.

Mum's gotta go. Again, I set my hand on Daiki's head and pivoted past him to get back to the living room. I grabbed my mobile phone and put it in my handbag, and checked to make sure that the gas was turned off. Daiki shuffled across the floor in his socks, not letting me out of his sight. As before, he was completely expressionless. *Hey, what is up with you tonight? What is it?* I got down on my knees, careful not to snag the hem of my dress, and grabbed Daiki by both of his arms. That was when I finally noticed it. Daiki wasn't stone-faced. He was trying to keep himself from crying.

I looked up at the clock. 5:10. It wasn't as if this was the first time we were leaving Daiki alone by himself. And my husband was going to be home from work by 7:00. Daiki was going to be home alone for less than two hours—not a big deal. And actually, just the previous day, Daiki had been looking forward to being left in charge of the place.

But now, Daiki's eyes were downcast, as he tugged on the elbow-length sleeves of my bolero jacket. *What is it?* I didn't have any other words at my disposal, so I just kept repeating the same thing. I gently disentangled his fingers from my sleeves, held his hands tightly in my own and looked him in the eye to ask him again, *What is it?* This time, Daiki mumbled, "Mum, don't leave me." Tears dripped from his big, imploring eyes. Because he was facing down, his tears fell directly to the floor, plopping down in front of my knees—or rather, in front of the hem of my polyester dress, which covered my knees and bunched up as I kneeled. I stood up and pulled out my mobile phone. *I might be late,* I texted one of the girls who would probably be there.

But Daiki simply wouldn't tell me what this was all about. *What is it? Did you get into a fight with one of your friends?* I asked. *Are you being bullied?* I asked. But he just shook his head and, doing everything he could to keep from breaking down into sobs, he let the tears flow quietly.

It was really rare for him to be in such a state. After entering elementary school, he had suddenly started acting like a little adult. Normally, he would be trying either to make me laugh or to get a rise out of me. I texted my friend again. *Sorry, I might be really late. I have a kid here who doesn't want to be left alone. Can you pass this on to whoever is organizing?*

I guided Daiki over to the kitchen table. He grabbed the backrest of my chair and would not let go. I thought that he might be ill and took his temperature just in case, but everything was normal. *Listen, I don't have to go out tonight,* I told him. It was sort of a trial balloon, but I was starting to think it was really true. This is what it means to have kids. I didn't feel even a hint of regret or annoyance. On the contrary, this was fulfilling. I handed a tissue box to Daiki and said to him, *I was looking forward to going out, but you're more important to me than any of that.*

A text came in to my phone. It was from my friend: AWFULLY HARD BEING A MUM. DO WHAT YOU HAVE TO DO, MIKA. I'LL RELAY YOUR MESSAGE. EVERYONE WANTS TO SEE YOU WHENEVER YOU CAN MAKE IT!

Daiki blew his nose. Then, with the tissue still covering his mouth, he mumbled very softly, "When Dad comes home, you can go." *Why can't I go before then,* I asked, and a single perfect teardrop flowed from his eyes. *Because you'll be lonely here all by yourself*, I said, babying him just a little. After what appeared to be a brief inner struggle, Daiki nodded, almost imperceptibly, and blew his nose again.

The wedding reception was scheduled to start at 7:00, and 7:00 is when I finally left home. By the time I got to the venue, it was after 8:30. A buffet had been laid out along the wall across from the entrance, but what was left in the platters qualified less as "dinner" than as "dirty dishes". But we were all paying 6,000 yen regardless. No one was going to knock it down to 3,000 yen for me because I got there late.

My old classmates had piled some carbonara and three kinds of cake on a little plate and set it aside for me. "Oh, and, Mika, there are still two slices of pizza left over here." That plate made its way around the table to join the other in front of me. When the draft beer that I ordered arrived, all of my friends around the table grabbed whatever glass was closest to them to toast my arrival, some that had only half-melted ice in them, some that were clearly not their own. "Here we go... *kanpai*! Glad you finally made it, Mika!" I was thirsty. It was a mid-sized mug, but I immediately downed half of it.

I was hungry. I took a bite of the carbonara. The sauce had got clumpy and cold, to the point that it almost seemed colder than the beer I was drinking, and when the flash of a digital camera went off nearby, the fat of the bacon shimmered disgustingly. The pizza had been set on the same plate as a salad, and its thin crust was soppy with the dressing. The only thing remotely edible was the cake.

About half of the guests had got up from their tables and begun to mill around. The lighting in the room was low to begin with, but now it was even darker with all of the standing bodies surrounding me. I caught a glimpse of the bride among the mingling crowd. I was taken aback for a second thinking she was naked, but then someone moved aside and I saw that she was wearing a strapless wedding dress. I made short work of the cake and ordered another beer. I retrieved my mobile phone and flipped it open to find that I had just one bar of reception.

"Everything OK with your kid?" someone asked. *Yeah*, I said, watching my phone go out of range and then back to one bar. I set it on my lap. *I was kind of surprised. Usually, he's not the type to wig out at something like this.*

In the end, I paid 6,000 yen to put one and a half beers and three bite-sized samples of cake in my stomach. And I got a photo with the bride when I pushed my way through the crowd. The party ended shortly after 9:00. My classmates were making noise about an after-party. There were three hours before the last train. I was a little torn. When my husband got home, he had been surprised to find me there, and when I filled him in on the situation, he had said, "I'll handle it. Just leave Daiki to me." Once I finally got here, I received a lot of compliments on my outfit, and on my figure. It made a girl want to stay around longer. But I was worried about Daiki. As the conversation about where to go next stalled, I slipped away from the group and called our home phone. My husband didn't come to the phone, and neither did Daiki. I grew more unsettled the longer it kept ringing. I hung up when it went past ten rings. I pushed the redial button. They had to be at home now. But again, no one picked up. I clutched the phone in my hand and took a deep breath. Perhaps the two of them had gone out to the convenience store together or something. I tried my husband's mobile phone. I should have just started with his mobile, I told myself, waiting for my husband to pick up. After fourteen rings, it went to voicemail. I hung up and called again. I did this three or four times before my friends called out to me: "Mika, we're on the move."

I started to turn towards them, but just then, I heard someone else call my name. It was coming from the phone in my hand. I quickly brought it up to my ear. It was my husband, but all that I could hear was Daiki's sobbing in the background. My friends couldn't help but smile as they watched me. They waved to catch my attention.

*   *   *

My husband hadn't picked up the phone because Daiki didn't want him to. Daiki was wailing, almost like an animal, but my husband somehow managed to explain it to me.

"The phone seems to be setting him off," he said in a slow, loud voice. This was followed immediately by Daiki's crying more intensely, more painfully. My husband was trying to hand the phone over to Daiki. *Daiki*, I called out, turning away from my friends and raising my voice. *Daiki, it's Mum, Daiki.* The line went dead. When I called again, it went straight to voicemail. *I'm heading home now*, I texted my husband.

While I was on the train, I received a reply from my husband. Daiki hadn't said a word during dinner or in the bathtub, but finally he couldn't hold out any longer. My husband had put Daiki on his lap and the explanation had come out in bits and pieces. He sent me the story as he had reconstructed it.

That afternoon, in the pocket playground, Daiki had had a curse laid on him. The lore of the park was, you didn't want to be there at 4:44. Even if you were in a group of people, it was safest to get out before the clock hit 4:44. And anyone who happened to be the only kid in the park at 4:44 would definitely be cursed. Which explained why every day, seconds before the clock hit 4:44, children would run screaming out of the park. But Daiki had screwed up. He had been high up on the climbing frame when he realized too late that the minute was near. In a panic, he had jumped down to make up for lost time, but he found himself down on his knees as a bolt of pain shot through his legs. By the time he got to his feet again, his friends were gone and the clock hands were exactly at 4:44. He ran for dear life down the path, but when he reached the front of the shuttered bedding shop, he was met by taunts from his friends. "Bye, Daiki," they said. "You've been cursed."

It was an established fact that the curse was coming from the ghost of a little girl. What her story was, no one knew, but everybody knew the ghost of a girl haunted the pocket playground. At night she would appear, playing by herself on the sphere of the climbing frame, her long hair all tangled in the night breeze. During the day she would sleep, but at 4:44 she would awaken in a flash and curse any kid she found there.

What was her curse like? Well, the ghost waits for evening, when her powers are at their peak, and then she calls the victim's house. When the kid picks up, she says, "Hey, come out to the pocket playground and play." Naturally, the kid will say, "No way!" and hang up. After a bit, the phone will ring again. The girl's voice will say, slightly more insistently, "Come out to the pocket playground." "No way!"

the kid will say, and hang up. And after a bit the phone will ring again. "Come out to the pocket playground. I'll pick you up and we can go together."

"Come out to the pocket playground. I'm almost at your door."

"Come out to the pocket playground. Come on, open up, come on."

The very last time she speaks, the line is, "Now let's go over to the pocket playground together."

What happens after that, nobody knows. Any kid who allows the ghost to take him by the hand and lead him to the pocket playground is sure to die, so the legend doesn't have much to say about what happens next.

The train was full, and there was no place to sit. I stood next to a door, leaning against the glass panel. Through my reflection in the glass, I looked at the darkness beyond—and at the lights of the apartment buildings, and street lights, and the headlights of cars waiting at the crossings that slashed across my image. When I was about Daiki's age I would freak out at things like this, too. But now all I could feel was anger at the nastiness behind this utterly unexceptional, half-baked ghost story. What kind of family did a kid have to come from to spread this kind of nonsense? And why would kids be so stuck on a place that had such a creepy story attached to it?

My eyes fixed on the text coming in from my husband: I TOLD HIM OVER AND OVER THAT THE PHONE CALLS WERE MUMMY TRYING TO GET IN TOUCH WITH US, BUT DAIKI REFUSES TO BELIEVE IT. It was really outrageous, scaring poor Daiki like this. The characters on the mobile phone screen were swimming now, and I could feel a hot, grainy lump rising in the back of my throat. I struggled to focus on the words in front of me. I was overcome by a mixture of rage and inebriation. I felt that I had to protect Daiki. Children are horrible. Two days from now, Daiki would of course be alive and well, and he would show up at school perfectly fine, but that didn't mean the other children would all gather around to congratulate him on escaping the jaws of death. They might even start bullying him. Daiki, the cursed child.

When the front door opened with a creak, Daiki threw himself around my husband's body and shrieked in terror, but when he saw it was me, the tension finally seemed to break. Daiki's face and even his pajamas were damp with his tears, but without hesitating I threw my arms around him, evening dress be damned. If I just wash it a little wherever it gets dirty, it will be good as new, I figured. It wasn't like it was silk or anything. Daiki put his arms around my neck, buried his face in my shoulder and quietly sobbed.

"I'm glad you're back," my husband said with a grim smile. "The little man still needs his mama first and foremost."

The back of Daiki's head was warm. I tousled his thick hair, careful not to knot it around my fingers. *Mummy's not going to let anything happen to you, OK*, I said to him. Daiki looked up at me, a trace of a smile on his face.

"I'm glad you're back," my husband said again, and let out a big yawn.

I visualized the faces of the friends I had just been with. *My kid is having a tough time*, I had said by way of a farewell. They all had kind things to say to console me: "Aw, you just got here," and "You're such a good mother, aren't you," and "It's a tough job." They all were sympathizing with me. And although I didn't say it in so many words, I sympathized with them. It was a sympathy mingled with a warm feeling for the good old days. They were now the way I was long ago. "Long ago" meaning only seven or eight years prior, but back then I was just a happy-go-lucky girl who could think only about myself, make plans with only myself in mind, and pretty much do as I pleased. Everything was different now. Any question of what *I* wanted to do no longer factored into the equation. They had yet to discover how sweet that could be, what pride there was in it. My husband understood it, probably, but certainly not like I did.

I led Daiki to his bedroom and put him to bed. I picked up the model of the pocket playground, a Daiki original, from its customary position next to his pillow and moved it to his desk, so that I could sit down on his bed. Smoothing back his hair, I asked him gently, *Now who told you such a crazy story?* Daiki thought for a while, before replying, "Everybody."

OK, well, this girl ghost—what does she look like?

"I don't know. Just that she has long hair."

So nobody has actually seen her?

". . . I don't know. But she comes out. At night."

Hmm. And so this ghost has a working mobile phone?

"Well. . ."

I snorted. *Look, Daiki, the whole thing is crazy.* I loomed over him and tickled his armpits. Daiki squealed and laughed out loud. "Mum, your breath smells like beer."

But he stopped laughing right away. "Mum," he said, gripping my hands. His hands felt softer than usual; maybe they were waterlogged from wiping his eyes all evening. His eyes already were brimming again with a new round of tears. "Mum, even if the spirit doesn't come today, it might come tomorrow. And if it doesn't come tomorrow, it might come the day after tomorrow."

I could picture vividly how Daiki's classmates would torture him saying things just like that. *Daiki, listen to me,*

OK? I wrapped his hands in both of my own. *If anyone tries to tell you that, you just tell them that the ghost and this curse are made-up stories. There is no such thing as a ghost of a girl. So nothing is coming to get you tonight, or tomorrow night, or the night after that, or anytime after that. Absolutely nothing is coming. You know who believes stories like that? Preschoolers,* I pronounced with all the authority I could muster.

But Daiki still looked at me uneasily. "But how do you know it isn't true, Mum?" he asked, in a small, pained voice. "How do you know it's a lie? How do you know she's not there? How do you absolutely, positively know she's not there? Can you prove it, Mum?" To my surprise, his voice grew insistent, and towards the end the stubborn little guy sounded downright unhappy with me. Daiki blinked slowly, looking straight up at me, his gaze never once wavering. His well of tears seemed to have run dry.

I was cold. The tips of my fingers and toes were icy with a chill like loneliness. If I weren't hunched forward with my chin down between my collarbones, I would have started shivering here and now. The back of my throat still felt gritty, and here, too, the cold had descended. And yet, despite all that, somehow my chest was warm.

I've got it, I said. *Get up, Daiki, Mum's going to prove it to you. I am going to take away all of your worries, Daiki.*

Daiki's confidence was suddenly shaken. His gaze lost its steeliness, and the furrow in his brow and the clench of his jaw softened. I sat up straight and stood up. Our hands, gripping one another so tightly, fell apart of their own accord. *It's all right, Daiki, leave it to me. We are going to settle this once and for all.*

Daiki licked his lip and bit down on it. Silently I watched him do this. At last he said, "OK," in the smallest of voices. He flipped over his duvet, slid his feet down to the floor and took hold of my outstretched hand.

I poked my head into our bedroom, where my husband was snoring peacefully. I was still in my dress and my bolero, so naturally I had to put my gold T-strap pumps back on to go with the outfit. Daiki, still in his pajamas, put on his trainers.

I leaned forward until my lips were right next to Daiki's ear, and whispered, *Now let's go over to the pocket playground together.* Daiki said nothing, but gripped my hand so fiercely that it cut off my circulation. It was the middle of the night, so I unlocked the door and pushed it open as quietly as I could so as not to bother any of our neighbours. At just that moment, the wind blew my hair in a tangle across my face, and in an instant the world before me went dark.

KAORI FUJINO

NAILS AND
EYES

KAZUSHIGE ABE

NIPPONIA
NIPPON

NATSUKO IMAMURA
AUTHOR OF THE WOMAN IN THE PURPLE SKIRT

THIS IS AMIKO,
DO YOU COPY?

NISHIOKA KYŌDAI

KAFKA

TOH ENJOE

HARLEQUIN
BUTTERFLY

KUMI KIMURA

SOMEONE
TO WATCH
OVER YOU